ANa StiLWeLL

MySteRies of the MaNSioN

J.W. JeNKiNS

GreenTree Publishers
Newnan, GA

Ana Stilwell - Mysteries of the Mansion

The characters and events of this book are fictitious. Any similarity to real persons, living or dead, is coincidental and not intended by the author.

Printed in the United States of America

ISBN-13: 978-1-944483-30-2

Follow J. W. Jenkins on social media:

Facebook: Ana-Stilwell-1981457255307418

Website: www.AnaStilwell.com

Email: Anastilwell2019@gmail.com

Greentree Publishers:
www.greentreepublishers.com

Dedication

It is with great joy that I dedicate *Ana Stilwell: Mysteries of the Mansion* to our grandchildren: Mackenna, Nathan, Katie, T.J., Maggie, Caroline, Davis, Amy, Charlotte, Bethany, and Christian. I pray they will someday enjoy reading all of my *Ana Stilwell* books to their children and grandchildren.

Special Thanks

My precious wife, Pam, helped me every step of the way. She listened patiently as I read out loud and offered great suggestions and ideas.

June Black, Jayden Pope, Tabea Hahn, Diana Fowler, Steven and Susan Jett offered essential editing assistance and many insightful comments, as did my ministry assistant, Cynthia Wilson. Many of those who enjoyed the first book, *Ana Stilwell's Greatest Adventure*, asked repeatedly when this second book would be available. Their encouragement kept me going.

Dr. Tim Riordan, of Greentree Publishers—an excellent, accomplished author—was, again, amazing! His constant attention to detail, style, knowledge of the whole process of writing and publishing a book, and encouragement was essential!

ANa StiLWeLL

MySterieS oF tHe MaNSioN

By J. W. JeNKiNS

FLaSHbacK - DeceMber 23, 1996

Multi-millionaire Rudolph Mason Griffin sat gazing at the huge portrait on the wall of his study—a painting of his family at the happiest time of his life. His wife, Beatrice, was so beautiful then, and his son, Lewis, was so young and alive. He remembered standing in front of the mansion, while the photographer focused the camera. A split-second before the photo was taken, he had heard a noise. Turning to his right, he saw the head of Lewis' tortoise, Ricky, poking out of the bushes. Although other photos were made that day, that was the one they had chosen for the painting. Griffin smiled. It was one of his fondest memories and guided his most serious decisions.

He turned his attention to the one-page document lying on the desk in front of him—his Last Will and Testament. Beatrice and Lewis had been dead for years. After searching the world, he was positive that he had no living heirs—no one to inherit his estate and fortune. He was 81 years old and had put off writing a new will for too long. He read it one last time, breathed a deep sigh, and signed it. Attorney, Lawrence Hill, was standing behind him—grinning. He had convinced Lewistowne's richest citizen to leave everything, simply, to "the bearer of the will." He knew that Griffin had been living like a hermit in the mansion for years, which probably meant that he didn't know or trust anyone well enough to appoint them as his heir.

"This way," Hill had told him, "you can just leave it up to God."

Griffin watched as his attorney applied the Notary Public seal and signed his name across it. Hill pointed to the insanely valuable piece of paper lying on the table. "All we need now is someone to witness our signatures," he explained. Griffin summoned his butler, Arnold Buttons, who entered, signed the document without reading it, and left. Lawrence Hill carefully printed the butler's name beneath the signature and dated it.

"Is that it?" Griffin asked.

"Yes sir. That's it. Our signatures, the date, and the seal make it official."

"Then it's done," he sighed. Rudolph Griffin picked up the document and examined everything one last time. "It's finally done." He inserted the will into a large envelope and then slid the envelope into an expensive leather portfolio. Griffin stood up and held out his hand toward Hill. "Thank you for helping me take care of this."

"Thank you for putting your trust in us," Hill shook his hand, "and please, if we can be of any further assistance, don't hesitate to call."

Griffin walked over and opened the door. "Come, it's late," he said.

The two of them exited the study, strolled through the magnificent hall and up the three wide steps to the main entrance. Not wanting to disturb the old butler again, Griffin unlocked and opened the gorgeous front door. He led the way out on to the front veranda. "Good night, Mr. Hill, and, once again, thank you."

"It was my pleasure," he replied and forced a smirky-looking grin. "Now, don't forget to put that will in a safe place," he leaned in and lightly patted Griffin's forearm. "And don't forget where you put it!"

Rudolph Griffin didn't respond. He watched as the much younger attorney turned, nimbly made his way down the front steps and strutted toward his automobile. He stood there until the rear-lights of Hill's vehicle disappeared into the night. "I promise you, young man, I won't forget anything about this night."

Griffin returned to his study and closed the door behind him. He sealed the portfolio away in the one place where he knew it would be safe. Standing once again before the family portrait, he glanced down at the grotesque head of his dead son's beloved pet. "Okay, Ricky, it's up to you now. Be sure to pick out the right person."

* * * * *

Three years later, Rudolph Griffin was pronounced dead by the county coroner. According to the record, he "died of natural causes in his sleep." His casket was never opened. It was placed in the ornate mausoleum on the grounds of the estate next to his beloved wife and son. During a bizarre settlement hearing that followed, attorney Lawrence Hill testified in public, that he and Griffin had created a valid last will, which the millionaire kept in his possession. The police made a very thorough search of the mansion but never found it. The estate was closed, and the massive entrance gates were chain locked. As the years passed, the will remained hidden in the enormous, abandoned mansion...until eleven-year old Ana Stilwell figured out where it was.

* * * * *

Five Months ago. With the leather portfolio containing the will tucked safely under her arm, Ana left the study and hurried through the abandoned mansion to the secret door in the rear hallway. It was still standing slightly open, just like she had left it. As soon as she saw it, however, a frightening thought surfaced in her mind.

It sure is a good thing that Lawrence Hill never came down this hall while I was in here. There's no way he could have missed seeing this.

Upon reaching the door, she was careful not to disturb the cobwebs as she pushed it open enough to slip through. Carefully, she stepped out of the trail of tracks in the dust and into the hidden passageway. Ana clicked on her flashlight. Reaching up, she felt the notch on the inside of the door frame and pulled it shut behind her. It didn't make a sound.

Okay, let's get out of here!

She made her way along the narrow hall and down the long flight of steps to the tunnel below. Using the skeleton key, Ana unlocked the massive wooden door, walked through, and locked it behind her. Seconds later she entered the large room and shined her flashlight at the profile of a man's head etched into the red clay wall.

"Look Mr. Rudolph! I found it!" She held up the portfolio. "Thank you for all the clues you left behind...and for the key!" Ana held it up in the air and then stuck it in her left pants pocket. She moved closer to the image. "Ricky is still alive." Ana swallowed hard. "I'll do my best to take care of him." Tears began to well up in the bottom of her eyes. She wiped her face with her sleeve and sniffed. "I'd better get home now. Bye!"

Making her way down the long, dark tunnel that led to the secret door at the creek, Ana picked up the pace, when she glimpsed the opening in the distance. Finally, back at the entrance, she removed the rock wedge from under the door, tossed it on the floor, and crawled out of the tunnel.

"Fresh air. Boy, does that smell good!" Ana stood up straight and carefully slid along the surface of the huge boulder. Using her right hand, she pushed the small, cleverly concealed stone entrance door shut.

Ker-clunk!

The sound of the hidden lever in the crevice to her left reminded her of the other lever she had discovered on the inside of the tunnel.

I need to make sure that one works, too.

Ana shook her head. "Why? Why worry about that now? I've got the will! That's all that matters!" Clutching the precious cargo under her arm, she carefully made her way up the creek to the place where large, flat rocks enabled her to cross over. Safely on the other side, the breath she had been holding for some time came rushing out. Ana rolled her eyes, looked upward, and saw the old stone wall above the massive boulders.

Glancing down at Rudolph Griffin's portfolio in

 her hands, she noticed the initials, *R.M.G.* engraved into the beautiful, dark leather. The sounds of the creek rushing by at her feet caused her to look up and think about the challenging trip back.

The last thing I need to do is drop this in the water!

She tried tucking it under each arm but knew she couldn't carry the will and keep her balance at the same time. After a couple of seconds, she snickered, "I've got it!" Pulling out her sweater, she jammed the portfolio up underneath it in front of her chest. Then she tucked her sweater into her jeans.

Ana leaned over and wiggled. "I'm glad no one is here to see me. I look like Sponge-Bob Square Pants!" she laughed and gazed up the creek. "Okay, let's see if this is going to work." After several jumps, she felt sure that her prize would remain securely in place.

Okay, Anastasia. You've got plenty of time. Just take it nice and easy.

A half-an-hour later, she reached her backyard and removed the will from underneath her sweater. Instead of going in the house, she circled around to the right between it and the garage. Just as she expected, her father wasn't home yet, and the car that belonged to her mother's old high school friend was still in the driveway. While making her way up the creek, she had decided—if it was possible—to go directly to Dr. David Barnes, the pastor of her church. She trusted him. Ana remembered that he had once explained in a sermon, that, as a pastor, he was "duty bound before God" to keep the stuff people told him a complete secret—unless, of course, they had broken the law.

The church was only a couple of blocks past her school, so it wasn't that far of a walk. Ana made sure to always keep the portfolio as out-of-sight of passing cars as possible. She got to her school and kept walking, being careful to not run. Ana kept her eyes lowered and directed at the sidewalk in front of her.

There's no sense drawing attention to myself.

She came to an intersection and knew that the church building was located down the street to her right. Just to be sure, though, Ana raised her head to check the street name on the sign. Out of the corner of her eye, she noticed a silver BMW roll to a stop on the opposite side of the intersection. She glanced at the driver and recognized him immediately.

It's Lawrence Hill!

Instantly bowing her head, she began slowly moving away from the intersection in the direction of the church. Ana squinted her eyes as she walked and prayed. When she asked Jesus to protect her and the will, she carefully slid it from underneath her right arm to in front of her chest. Ana crossed her arms around it—like she often did when carrying her schoolbooks—and finished her prayer.

Straining to detect the sound of the car's engine, her curiosity finally got the better of her. She pulled out her cell phone and held it up in front of her face, using the reflection in the screen like a mirror. Ana adjusted it to see behind her and her heart almost stopped. He was still there. Ana lowered the phone and tapped on the screen, like she was making a call.

What are you waiting on?

After a few seconds, she raised it up again. He was staring straight at her. Ana began shaking all over.

What is wrong with you? For crying out loud! I'm just some little girl walking down the sidewalk. I'm nobody! Just ignore me! Why don't you leave?

Suddenly the engine roared to life. Ana watched as the car crossed the intersection and sped away.

"Praise the Lord!" Ana breathed a sigh of relief and continued making her way down the sidewalk.

I wonder if he's headed back to the mansion. It's a good thing I'm not still inside. And it's a very good thing that he doesn't know who I am. Ana rubbed the leather portfolio she was carrying. *Or what I've found.*

She didn't think about it being late Friday afternoon and that the church office was already closed. Two cars were in the parking lot near the door and Ana hoped one of them belonged to the pastor. She peeked through the glass door and pressed the buzzer. After a couple of seconds, she pressed it again. Ana stepped back and looked around to see if anyone was outside. Returning to the window, she peered into the darkness of the hall again.

Where is he?

Ana was about to press the door buzzer again, when a light came on. She smiled as she saw her pastor coming toward her.

"Thank you, Lord Jesus!"

He unlocked the door and recognized her immediately, "Well, hello there, Ana. What brings you here this afternoon? You're not in trouble, are you?"

"No sir. I just need to show you something that I found." Ana held up the portfolio and noticed the church's building manager, Mr. Binkley, making his way toward them.

"Is there a problem, Dr. Barnes?" he called.

"No, Fred, I don't think so. I've got it," the pastor motioned for Ana to come inside. "Just stay close, please, until I can find out what's going on."

"Yes sir."

"Let's go to my office Ana," he said kindly and led the way. She followed him down the hall. Several workrooms branched off the main reception area. Dr. Barnes opened the door to his study. "Come on in and have a seat." He closed the door behind her and smiled at the building manager through the glass. Mr. Binkley waved and leaned against the wall, where he could see them but couldn't hear what was being said. Ana saw a dark wooden conference table with several chairs around it and took a seat. The pastor didn't sit in his large desk chair, but rather sat down across the table from her. "Okay, Ana," he smiled, "What's this all about?"

"This." She laid the expensive, leather portfolio on the table and opened it up. Carefully, she pulled out the large envelope, undid the metal clasp and opened it. Finally, she removed the will and slid it across the table in his direction. "This is why I'm here." The pastor picked up the one-page document and began reading.

"Oh, my!" he put his hand over his mouth and kept reading. His eyes grew larger the further he read. Ana watched him and could tell he was reading it through again, just to be sure.

He finally placed the will back on the table and stared at her. "Wow."

"What should I do?" Ana's voice was quivering.

Dr. Barnes managed a weak smile. "Well, this is, literally, way above my pay grade. We better pray and ask God for wisdom." Ana agreed and bowed her head. After the prayer, they were able to get in touch with her parents and then phoned Lewistowne's Chief of Police. The pastor assured everyone that Ana was fine. After ending his call to the chief, he checked his contacts and tapped in another number.

"I think you're going to need a lawyer," he looked at her and explained, "someone who understands finances, real estate, and how to guide you through what's going to happen." Ana nodded, but didn't reply. He pressed the speaker phone button, so they both could listen. The other phone rang and rang. Finally.

"Hello?"

"Chuck. This is David Barnes."

"Oh, hello, Pastor," Ana had heard her father talk about Chuck Switcher before. He was in his Bible Study class at church. "What's up? How can I help?" Ana listened as her pastor briefly explained the situation. When he finished, Chuck stated, "I'm on my way. I can be there in less than five minutes."

13

"Thanks Chuck. We're here in the church office. Mr. Binkley will let you in." He pressed the button to end the call.

"Thank you so much," Ana took a deep breath and let it out. She put her face into her hands and closed her eyes.

"I can't imagine what you've been through," offered Dr. Barnes kindly. Ana opened her eyes, glanced over at him, and shook her head.

"You wouldn't believe it, if I told you." She pointed at the will lying on the table. "It's still hard for me to believe that I actually found it."

"Have you taken a photo of it?" he asked. Ana sat up.

"What a great idea!" she exclaimed and yanked out her cell phone. Standing over the valuable document, she made a couple of photos with and without the flash. Zooming in on the result, Ana made sure that she could easily read the will. She glanced at her pastor. "Would you, please, make one of me holding it?" Dr. Barnes took several shots from different angles and handed Ana her phone. She sat back down without examining the results. "Thank you."

"Oh, you are quite welcome." They both just sat there for a whole minute without saying a word. Finally, Dr. Barnes broke the silence. "Would you like a bottle of water?"

"Oh, yes sir!"

"Coming right up!" He walked over to a cabinet in the paneled wall that concealed a small refrigerator. "I think I'll have one, too." As she watched him pull out the two bottles of water, she thought about the hidden door in the rear hallway of the mansion. He unscrewed the cap on one of them and handed it to her. "Here you go."

Ana thanked him and took a sip. "This is really good!" She kept drinking and almost drained it. She took a deep breath and laughed, "Wow, I was thirsty!"

Buzz!

"That's got to be Mr. Switcher." Dr. Barnes stood up and started toward the office door. Ana stood up, too, but didn't leave the room. Minutes later, the three of them were seated around the table.

"Before we start," Chuck Switcher smiled at Ana, "do you want me to act as your legal counsel?"

"Oh, yes. Please!" she breathed a deep sigh of relief. Chuck picked up the will and studied it.

"Oh, my goodness," he muttered. When he finished, he glanced at Ana and smiled. "Well, it looks pretty clear cut to me," he stated and then added, "but, of course, a judge will need to make the final decision." He leaned toward her and grinned "But the main thing is," he paused, "is that you are clearly the bearer of the will." He pointed to the words in the document. "That means you don't have to tell anyone how it came to be in your possession as long as you didn't do anything... illegal." Chuck glanced at Dr. Barnes and then back at Ana. "You didn't do anything you shouldn't have, did you?"

"No sir."

"Then there won't be any reason to worry. Right?" Chuck smiled.

"Right." Ana took another gulp of her water.

Before long, they were joined by Ana's parents and Lewistowne's Chief of Police, Buster Matthews. More chairs were brought into the pastor's office and placed around the table. Mr. Binkley was released to go home.

After brief introductions and an explanation by Dr. Barnes, Chief Matthews immediately made photos of the will, the envelope, and the leather portfolio. He made several photos of Ana holding the will and a group photo of everyone in the room with her holding the will. Each photo had a date stamp on it.

"Okay. That's done. Now I need to take your statement, Ana," he smiled and set up a small, digital recorder on the table. "Do you know what that means?"

"Yes sir," she nodded.

"Perfect," he said and scooted his chair next to hers. He began by stating all the necessary preliminary information, which included the date, time, and location. Then he asked Ana to state her name, age, and address. Her voice was shaking as she spoke. He pressed pause on the recorder.

"You're doing great, Ana," his voice was very deep, but kind. "Just tell the truth and you will be fine." Ana swallowed hard, glanced at her parents, her pastor, Chuck Switcher, and then back at the Chief of Police. "Okay. Let's continue," he pressed the record button again. "When and where did you find Rudolph Griffin's Last Will and Testament?" Ana let out a breath and gripped the arms of the chair.

"Today, uh, this afternoon in Mr. Griffin's mansion...in his study." Ana's answers came out in stages—like she was jumping from one rock to the next.

"How did you get into the Griffin mansion?" the police chief continued.

"I'd, uh, I'd rather not say," Ana's voice was shaking, "if...if I don't have to." She glanced over her shoulder at Chuck. He shook his head and smiled. Ana looked back at the Chief of Police, who was not smiling. She heard him clear his throat like he was going to say something and quickly added, "but I can tell you that I didn't break in. I...I had a key."

"You had a key?" her mother blurted out.

"Yes, ma'am," Ana spun around and stared at her. "I found it."

Chief Matthews sighed, pressed the pause button, and stared at Nancy Stilwell. "Please, ma'am. No interruptions. I only need Ana to speak at this time." Ana watched her mother silently mouth 'I'm sorry!' The police chief turned, looked back at Ana and re-started the recorder. "Your statement, Ana, is that you found a key that allowed you access into the Griffin mansion. Is that correct?"

"Yes sir."

"So, your testimony is that you did not break into the mansion. Is that correct?"

"Yes sir."

18

"Do you have the key with you?"

"Oh, yes sir!" Ana jumped up, dug into the pocket of her jeans and pulled out the skeleton key. Everyone in the room gasped, including Chief Matthews.

"Let the record show," he continued, "that Ana Stilwell is in possession of a key to the Griffin mansion."

"Where did you find it?" The serious tone of the chief's voice caused her to sit back down. He repeated the question, "Ana, where did you find the key?"

She stared down at the slender metal object in her hand. "That's…that's what I can't tell you. I can't tell anyone."

"What's wrong, Ana? Why can't you tell where you found the key?" probed the chief.

Ana swallowed and shook her head. She felt the tears coming. "I don't think he would want me to."

"Who, Ana? Who doesn't want you to tell?" Chief Matthews leaned forward in his chair.

Ana stared at him, with tears flowing down her cheeks. "Rudolph Griffin."

* * * * *

ONe MoNtH Ago. A court hearing was held, in which Lawrence Hill was summoned to testify and confirm that it was, in fact, his signature on the will. Judge Henry Murphy declared that eleven-year-old Anastasia Elisabeth Stilwell was the legal bearer of the Last Will and Testament of Rudolph Mason Griffin. She got everything! The enormous, ornate mansion on the huge estate, lots of very expensive stuff, massive amounts of stock in several companies and millions of dollars in cash.

The news spread, and reporters arrived from everywhere. At first, Ana agreed to talk to them. But when they asked her to reveal exactly *how* she had found the will—and they used every trick in the book to try and coax it out of her—she would seal her lips so tight together that you would have thought she'd used crazy glue. Why?

Ana Stilwell knew how to keep a secret.

CHapter ONe

"I am so glad we're finally going to get this place cleaned up!" Ana Stilwell stood on the front veranda of the huge Griffin mansion, gazing around at the overgrown, debris-covered estate that hadn't been touched in years. Chuck Switcher, her lawyer and personal financial advisor, didn't respond. Ana glanced over at him and saw that he was checking an incoming text message on his phone.

"That's Johnson's Lawn Service now," he smiled. "I'll drive out to the rear gate and let them in. If I think they can do the job, I'll give you a call, so that you can make the final decision." He hurried down the steps and headed toward his old Ford truck, that was parked next to her Mercedes.

"Chuck!" called Ana, "if you think they can handle it, please go ahead and hire them. I want them to get after it as soon as possible!"

"Yes, ma'am!" he waved with his hand but didn't stop to look back. Ana shook her head.

Ma'am. That sounds so weird, when people call me that...like I'm an old woman. Being rich sure does change things. People act so goofy...like they're scared or something.

As Ana watched Chuck's truck head toward the service entrance, she recalled the telephone conversation they had had with the lawn service, less than an hour before. Chuck had hit the speaker button on the phone, so Ana could listen in.

"Hello. This is Larry." She remembered thinking how young the voice on the other end of the call had sounded.

"Is this Johnson's Lawn Care?" Chuck had inquired.

"Yes sir. Can you hold a second?" Larry Johnson didn't wait for a response, but instead covered the phone with his hand and began yelling at someone outside to turn off a mower so that he could hear.

Chuck had also covered the phone with his hand and rolled his eyes at Ana. "Sure. No problem. We can wait," he said softly and then smiled. After a few seconds, the young lawn service owner was back.

"Sorry about that," Larry apologized. "Okay. Are you calling about an existing account? Or would you like to begin a new service?"

22

Chuck grinned at Ana. "We would like to begin a new service, please."

"All right. Just a moment and I'll get you all set up." Ana could hear more background noises coming from the phone. Larry Johnson had grown up in Lewistowne and, according to Chuck, had a very good reputation. After about thirty seconds he returned. "Okay. May I have your address, please?"

"Sure. It's 39 Griffin Avenue."

"39 Griff-in A-ve-nue." They could hear a pecking sound over the phone. It sounded like he was typing the address into a computer. Ana snickered at Chuck. "Okay. Got it. Let me just check your location on our map." Seconds passed. Finally, they heard him ask "Umm. Did you say 39 Griffin Avenue?" His voice sounded different—like there was a problem.

"Yes, that's correct," confirmed Chuck as he winked at Ana.

"Are you kidding me?" Larry Johnson's voice was quivering. Then it turned sarcastic. "Who is this? Is this some-kind-of-a joke? Bobby? Bobby? Is that you?"

Chuck waited a couple of seconds. "No, Mr. Johnson. I can assure you that this is not a joke and that I am not Bobby. This is Chuck Switcher. I am calling on behalf of Miss Ana

Stilwell, the new owner of the Griffin estate. We are interested in hiring you as our lawn service. You would need to begin with a complete clean-up of the grounds, which have been very neglected."

"Oh, my goodness!" he stuttered. "I mean, yes, yes. I would love to be your lawn service. Uh, I mean we. We would love to be your lawn service. When do you want me, uh, us, to start?"

"Well, we are at the estate right now. I realize it's extremely short notice, but would it be possible for you to come over and discuss what needs to be done this afternoon? Miss Stilwell wants you to begin as soon as possible."

"Sure! No problem!" Larry was almost shouting. "It'll take me fifteen minutes, tops, to get there. I can be there by...four o'clock. Is that okay?"

"That will be perfect. Just come to the rear service entrance. Do you know where that is?"

"No problem. I'll find it."

"Great," said Chuck, "Just send me a text when you arrive at four."

"4:00 p.m. Got it! I'll be there. I'm leaving right now. Thank you. Thank you so much."

From the front terrace, Ana allowed her gaze to slowly sweep to the right, surveying what she could see of the vast estate. She let out another sigh.

I hope he can handle it. There is so much to do.

"I've finished my rounds. Are you about ready to go?" Ana recognized the deep voice of her huge personal bodyguard, Andrew Collins, who had walked up from behind. She smiled and turned around to respond to him, but didn't, because she caught a glimpse of her eight-year-old brother coming around the corner of the mansion.

"You have got to be kidding me!" she cried and ran down the front steps in his direction. "Connor!" she screamed. Andrew spun around to see why she was suddenly so upset and quickly covered his mouth to hide his amusement. "Connor! Stop teasing Ricky!" she shouted. "I mean it!"

"But he likes it!" he laughed. He was riding on top of Ana's huge pet tortoise, dangling a large, juicy carrot from the end of a long stick. The ancient reptile was straining to bite the treat just inches from its nose.

"If you don't quit it right now, I'll banish you from the estate!" Ana was using one of the old words they had learned in English class at school the week before.

Connor stopped and turned toward his sister. Ana saw the puzzled expression on his face. "What's *banish* mean?"

"It means that you will never, ever get to come over here again—for the rest of your life! Now, get down off him! And give him that carrot you've been teasing him with!"

"Oh, all right." Connor slid off the back of the massive shell. Ana stood with her arms crossed and watched as her brother untied the carrot and tossed it on the ground. "Happy now?"

"Yes. Thank you. Ricky doesn't deserve to be treated like that."

The two of them watched as the enormous creature scooped up the prize. He slowly turned his head and gazed at them. The end of the carrot was sticking out of the corner of his mouth, bobbing up and down as he chewed on it. The expression on his face was hilarious. Ana quickly grabbed her cell phone, and Ricky held the pose.

"How old do you think he is?" asked Connor.

"I don't know." She mumbled without looking at him and snapped another photo.

"I'll bet he's a hundred years old."

"Um, huh. Maybe," Ana used her fingers to enlarge the photo on her phone. "Just look at that face!" She showed it to her brother.

Connor laughed, "I think he likes getting his picture made."

Ana didn't respond. Her brother's comment triggered a memory of the first photo she had ever seen of Ricky. The one of Lewis Griffin on top of the tortoise that was made on the Galapagos Islands many years before she was born. Ana stared at the photo on her phone and thought about the Griffin family: Lewis, Beatrice, and Mr. Rudolph. She walked over and began rubbing Ricky lovingly on the head. She saw the tortoise close its eyes and felt him press his head upward into the warmth of her palm. Ana blinked her eyes, trying not to cry.

Connor stared at his older sister. "Ana? Are you all right? What's wrong?"

She looked away and wiped her face on her sleeve. "You wouldn't understand."

Chapter Two

After school, Ana perched on the built-in seat
of the bay window in her bedroom. She
lowered her chin to the top of her knees and
gazed out the window. A girl, that looked to be
about her same age, was talking on her cell
phone and slowly making her way down the
sidewalk in front of their house. The weather
wasn't too cold to play outside, but then again,
it had been months since Ana had any time to
just *play*. She closed her eyes and rested the
side of her head on her knees, trying to recall
how her life used to be. She missed being able
to be alone, like down at the creek behind their
house... at her favorite spot.

Life was so normal, back then.

That thought reminded her of the day she had
decided to explore farther down the creek—the
first time she had seen the wall—and later
learned from her father about the abandoned
Griffin Estate. She recalled the thrill of finding
the secret door in the huge boulder and the
tunnel.

Like the pages of a book being flipped by the wind, her thoughts progressed through the incredible series of events that had followed—every detail, every clue, every glorious discovery and every petrifying fear. She remembered how it felt finally opening the hidden safe and holding Rudolph Griffin's lost will in her hands. She recalled how people in the courtroom had cheered when the judge announced that she would get it all... and the look on Lawrence Hill's face. Ana opened her eyes and glanced out the window. The other girl was gone.

I wonder who she was?

Ana closed her eyes again. Her thoughts shifted aimlessly back and forth—from the mansion and huge estate that she now had to take care of, to the Griffins, to Chuck and Andrew, to her mom and dad, to Connor, to school, to—ugh! Skylar Perkins, to—yes! Carter Hudson, to Sunday School, to her amazing teacher, to church... Thinking about church reminded her that she ought to pray.

Dear God, please let me know what I need to do. Please don't let me make a mistake or do something stupid. I know You've got this, and I know I'm not supposed to worry, but please show me—help me make good decisions. Help me to—

"Chuck's here!"

Ana's head shot up. Her younger brother was yelling at the top of his lungs from the downstairs hallway.

"Chuck's here! Everybody! Chuck's here!"

Good grief. What a loudmouth!

Ana closed her eyes again. *Dear God, please help me to not strangle my little brother.* She wanted to snicker but then remembered that she was praying. *And remind me that he is just excited and help me to love him... like You do. Amen.*

She and her mother arrived in the downstairs hallway at about the same time. Connor was standing in the doorway pointing at Chuck Switcher, who had parked his car in front of the house and was coming up the front walkway.

"You don't need to call him Chuck. You need to refer to him as Mr. Switcher." Ana's mother corrected as she walked past Connor to the door.

"Would you please show some respect?" chided Ana from directly behind her mother.

"But you call him Chuck, so why can't I?" Ana turned around to argue with her brother, when she saw Andrew silently gliding down the hall toward him.

"You need to be quiet." Andrew's deep voice, inches away from Connor's head, caused him to spin around, almost ramming his nose into the bodyguard's massive form. Andrew caught him just in time, picked him up, and held him tightly in his grasp. "You got that, Master Stilwell?"

"Yes, sir." Connor fell limp. Ana was thankful for Andrew's calming effect on her rambunctious younger brother. She also knew that he liked it when her bodyguard called him *Master Stilwell.*

Every Friday afternoon, right after school, Chuck met with Ana and her parents, Nancy and Ronnie Stilwell, who had been appointed as the trustees of her fortune. Andrew was never in the living room during the meeting, because his job was to make sure Connor stayed in the kitchen and didn't try to listen through the door.

"As we all know, the Griffin fortune was vast." Chuck removed a stack of stapled papers from his briefcase. "Ana, I'm still trying to locate everything you own." He handed everyone a copy of the latest financial statement. "According to the most current estimate, your fortune is now over $257 million dollars." Ana saw her mother swallow hard. Her father wiped his forehead with his hand. "I know it sounds crazy," Chuck continued, "but it seems like the more money you give away, the more money keeps flowing in." He picked up a two-page document and handed it to her. "Take this for example. It came in the mail today."

"What is it?" asked Ana.

"A quarterly dividend statement from a company in which you own shares of stock."

"What does that mean?"

"Well, when you own shares of stock in a company, sometimes the company pays you a dividend. You get money for each share of stock you own," Chuck explained.

"So, did they send me a check?"

"Well, no," he explained, "Rudolph Griffin decided not to receive a check each quarter, but instead instructed the company to reinvest the money—to buy more shares of stock." Ana could tell that Chuck was trying to keep it simple. "See right here?" he pointed with his finger to a line on the paper." This shows how many shares you own." He moved his finger across the page. "This shows how much the dividend was. This shows how many shares you bought with the dividend and..." He moved his finger again. "And, this shows how much all of the shares you own are worth now."

"$187,344 dollars and 73 cents?" She cried and stared up at him.

"$187,344 dollars and 73 cents." Chuck's tone was very businesslike.

"So, that's why you said the money just keeps flowing in?"

"Yes, ma'am." Chuck returned the statement to the envelope.

"Wow." Ana sat back in her seat.

"Chuck, when do you think we will finally know everything she owns?" asked her mother.

"That's a good question." He shook his head. "Rudolph Griffin kept his own financial matters to himself. He was obviously not very trusting of people. But I must say, he knew what he was doing."

Ana drummed her fingers on the arms of the dark leather chair. Chuck and her parents watched her. She was very selective in how she spent the money, in fact, she was downright picky.

"It's not really my fortune," she had told them. "Rudolph Griffin earned all this. He just left it to me, because I found his will. His son, Lewis, should have gotten everything, but he sacrificed his life to save others. So, I'm not ever going to waste one dime of it."

Even though finding the will had made her extremely wealthy, Ana had not bought one single thing for herself. But on this Friday, after Chuck was finished with his weekly status report, she spoke up.

"I want to change the name of the newspaper back to *The Lewistowne **Hero** News,*" She emphasized the word *Hero* and noted the shocked expression on everyone's face. "It was originally called *The Pineville Gazette,*" she explained, "but when Lewis died in the Vietnam War, they changed the name of the town and the newspaper to honor him." Ana paused. "After Rudolph Griffin died, the new owner removed the word *Hero* and made it just *The Lewistowne News.*" After a moment of silence, she added, "and I think that stinks."

The three adults in the room sat still without saying a word. Ana figured they were trying to digest what she had just told them. Chuck finally spoke.

"In order to change the name, Ana, you would need to own the newspaper," he explained. "Is that something you really want to do? Do you want to buy '*The Lewistowne News*'?"

Ana didn't hesitate. "Yes sir, I do."

"You might be forced to purchase the building and all the equipment," he added. "This is a big deal, Ana. And before we begin, I need to know how much you are prepared to spend."

Ana leaned forward and laid her small hands out flat on the table in front of her. She looked at her parents and then back at Chuck. "Whatever it takes!"

Chuck nodded. "Yes, ma'am. No problem. When do you want to buy it?"

"Tomorrow."

Chapter Three

It was 10:05 the next morning when Ana, Andrew, and Chuck strolled into the lobby of *The Lewistowne News.* No one else was in the room, except the receptionist, who was sitting behind a very modern-looking desk. She was talking on her cell phone when they entered. They politely waited for her to finish. Ana was standing with Andrew on her right and Chuck on her left. She noticed the name plate on the desk. *Ms. Amanda Plum.*

"Uh, honey, let me call you back," whispered the receptionist as she ended the call, and stood up. She studied the trio in front of her with an odd look on her face. Ana could tell that she was trying to figure out which one was the leader. She decided on Chuck.

"May I help you?"

Chuck didn't respond but instead motioned down at the young girl beside him. Ana stepped forward.

"Good morning, Ms. Plum. If it's possible, we would like to speak with the owner of the newspaper, please." The receptionist smirked, glanced back and forth at Andrew and Chuck who stood perfectly still, and then back down at Ana.

"And just who, may I ask, are you?"

"Oh, please forgive me, I'm Ana Stilwell." The smirk on the receptionist's face melted into an expression that you only see when someone suddenly realizes that they are in the presence of a lot of money.

"Oh. Miss Stilwell. Uh, I didn't recognize you. Please forgive me. I'll get Mr. Pressley at once!" she twirled around and stumbled over her chair. "Oh. How clumsy of me. Just a moment. I'll be right back. Please, wait here." She disappeared down the hall.

"It's quite all right," Ana called. "We've got plenty of time."

Seconds later, Winton Pressley hurried into the lobby but stopped in his tracks when he saw Ana and the two men with her. He cleared his throat and stroked the small, white beard in the middle of his chin. Ana recognized him immediately.

Oh, my goodness. He's the guy who was with Lawrence Hill on the sidewalk in front of the law office. He was also in the court room during the hearing, when Judge Murphy announced his ruling.

Ana recalled seeing his photo in the old newspapers. He was much younger then and had more hair, but it was him. The little beard in the middle of his chin gave him away.

I knew I had seen you somewhere before!

"Well, well! The famous Miss Stilwell," he announced and headed straight for her. Andrew instantly moved and blocked the way with his huge body.

"Sir, that's close enough!"

"What?" exclaimed Pressley and backed away. "I'm so sorry, I didn't mean to approach her without permission."

Chuck snickered, "Andrew, I think we can trust Mr. Pressley to not harm Miss Stilwell." Ana was grateful for her bodyguard's reaction, because it gave her time to compose herself and collect her thoughts.

This is the missing piece of the puzzle! This explains why you changed the name of the newspaper. You made sure to stop printing anything about the Griffins after the estate settlement hearing, when Hill revealed the existence of the will. Oh, my goodness! I'll bet you and Hill were in on this together! You did everything you could to cause people to forget about the will...but that didn't help you find it, did it?

She scrutinized the owner of *The Lewistowne News* from head to toe and grinned.

I'll bet you would like to strangle me.

"Thank you, Andrew." Unafraid, Ana stepped forward and stuck out her hand. "I apologize. He's very protective and, goodness knows, I need protection."

"Oh, no. It was my mistake, Miss Stilwell. Please accept my apology," offered Pressley. He cradled her small hand in both of his, caressed it gently and forced a smile. "So, what brings you to *The Lewistowne News* today? I can only hope you are here to give us an exclusive news story. You know what everyone is dying to know, myself included." A warning signal went off in Ana's head.

What a snake! You think I'm here to give you an interview, don't you? To tell you how I found the will. Well, aren't you going to be surprised?

Ana glanced at Chuck and nodded. "Miss Stilwell isn't here to give an interview but rather to make you an offer."

"Make me an offer?" the newspaper owner let go of her hand. His charming smile and pleasing tone were gone. "An offer? What kind of offer?"

"I want to buy your newspaper," declared Ana. Chuck had done the research and had informed her that it was worth, including everything, approximately four million dollars.

"B—B—Buy my newspaper?" he stammered, staring back and forth at the three faces in front of him. "Are you kidding me? Do you have any idea how much it's worth?"

"How much do you want for it?" Ana asked sternly. "I want to buy it all. The newspaper, equipment, building, everything. Just name your price." She noticed a small, thin stream of sweat snaking its way down the left cheek of the owner of *The Lewistowne News*.

Ana and Chuck were prepared for the meeting. They had considered how Winton Pressley might react—that he probably had no intentions of selling the paper. Ana knew now that he certainly wouldn't want to sell it to her—the little girl who had wrecked their schemes.

"But if he doesn't immediately turn you down flat," Chuck had explained earlier, "it might be because he doesn't want to lose face in front of you. That will be our one chance."

"What do you mean, Chuck?" she asked.

"He's arrogant. He might come up with some ridiculous price—much more than it's worth and much more than he thinks you'll be willing to pay. He could try to call your bluff."

They had discussed exactly what she should say and how to react if Pressley made her an offer. Now, everything was playing out just like they had imagined it might.

Ana saw Mr. Pressley puff out his chest and smirk at his receptionist, who was gnawing feverishly on one of her fingernails. Ana sensed what was about to happen and stifled the giggle that was straining desperately to bubble out.

I can't believe it. He's going to make me an offer!

Winton Pressley turned and stared at her. His lips formed a vicious, nasty sneer.

"Okay. All right, Miss Stilwell. I'll sell it to you...for ten million dollars!"

"Ten million?" Chuck exploded. "You can't be serious!" He turned and winked at Ana. "That's more than twice what it's worth. This is ridiculous!"

"Well, that's the price!" Pressley pounded his fist on the desk in front of Ms. Plum, who jumped like she had been shot. "And I demand that you write me a check for the whole amount right now! It's all or nothing." Again, he glanced around at Chuck, Andrew, and his receptionist. None of them were smiling. He then glared down at Ana. "Ten million dollars! Take it or leave it!" He sneered and stuck out his hand.

The conceited expression on his face was not long-lived.

Ana reached out, grabbed his hand, and shook it as hard as she could. "It's a deal, Mr. Pressley, I'll take it!" She kept shaking his hand and twisted to her right. "Chuck, would you please give Mr. Pressley the check for ten million?"

"Yes, ma'am," Chuck reached into his briefcase and grabbed a stack of checks. He quickly sifted through them and found the one for $10,000,000. "Here you go!" he said and handed him the check. Clearly stunned, Pressley took it in his trembling hand and just stood there staring back and forth at his name and the amount. Ana smiled.

He took it without thinking.

Chuck opened his briefcase and produced copies of a Bill of Sale—all ready to go. Only the amount needed to be filled in. Ana watched him write $10,000,000 in the spaces provided on the documents.

"We are all witnesses to the verbal contract that just took place. So, there's nothing else to be done, except to sign this Bill of Sale and close the deal," Chuck announced and held out a pen to the speechless publisher. "Unless, of course, you want to see us in court." Pressley stared at him, then at the pen, then at the check, then at Ana, and finally, back at Chuck. "Come on, Winton, you'll be able to tell everyone that you put one over on Ana Stilwell. You're getting more than twice what the paper's worth and we will pay all the closing costs! See?" He pointed to the highlighted blanks on the Bill of Sale. "Just sign here and here... and here on both copies. Winton Pressley mumbled something that no one understood and signed the papers. Chuck picked them up and examined the signatures. "Okay, now we need Ana's signatures and mine as her acting Power of Attorney." When they were done, Chuck made completely certain that everything was in order and handed Pressley his copy, then turned and gave Ana hers.

Ana looked down at the document. "Are we finished?"

"Yes, ma'am. It's official."

Ana reached over once more, grabbed Pressley's limp hand and shook it. "Thank you so much. It was nice doing business with you." He stood there staring at her like a deer caught in the headlights.

"Oh, and Winton," Chuck chimed in, "you have until 10 o'clock tonight to clean out your office. Don't worry about giving us your keys. Our team will be here in a few minutes to change all the locks and the security codes." Winton Pressley nodded, dropped his head, and headed down the hall toward his office.

Ana walked over to the seated, speechless receptionist and patted her hand.

"Isn't it exciting, Ms. Plum? Now you work for me."

* * * * *

Later that afternoon, Ana stood on top of one of the break-room tables in front of the assembled newspaper employees. She was holding a stack of note cards that she and Chuck had prepared. He and Ana's parents were standing on the ground next to the table. Ana motioned to Andrew.

"Quiet, please!" he commanded. Everyone immediately stopped talking and glared at him. It was so quiet that Ana could hear the clock ticking on the wall behind her.

"Thank you, Andrew," she said sweetly and began reading from the first card. "My name is Ana Stilwell. I am the new owner of this newspaper." The crowd in front of her began murmuring and gesturing with their hands. Ana motioned to Chuck. He walked in front of the table and held up a large framed photo of Lewis Griffin in his captain's uniform. Ana winked at Andrew.

"Quiet, please!" he bellowed, and the room fell silent again.

"Our city—Lewistowne—is named for Lewis Griffin, a captain in the Vietnam War, who sacrificed his life to save others." Chuck moved the photo from side to side so that everyone could see it. Flashes from cameras and cell phones captured the moment. "Years ago," she continued, "this newspaper's name was changed from *The Pineville Gazette* to *The Lewistowne Hero News* to honor him!" Ana emphasized the word hero. "Some years later the word, *Hero*, was removed. Today, I am adding it back! This newspaper will, once again, honor the sacrifice and memory of Captain Lewis Griffin! His photo and a brief explanation of who he was and how he died will be on the front page of every issue from now on. Is that clear?" Everyone nodded. "Are there any questions?" She gazed around the room. No one said a word. She looked over at Chuck and her parents. They smiled and she smiled back. Ana turned to face the crowd in front of her and lowered her note cards. "I promise you, that I will do everything I can to make you proud that you work here. May God bless you all." The room erupted with applause. Some cheered. Ana waved, and Andrew helped her down to the floor. He held careful watch as several took turns shaking her hand.

CHapter Four

When Ana and her family arrived at Lewistowne's First Baptist Church Sunday morning, everyone was buzzing about what had happened the day before. She noticed them staring and motioning in her direction. On the way to her Sunday School class, Ana stopped at the water fountain. She was still gulping down the refreshing stream, when Carter Hudson walked up behind her.

"Hey! Leave some for me," he quipped.

Ana lifted her head slightly and stopped drinking but kept her finger on the button. The water was still shooting out of the nozzle, as she turned and winked at him.

"I'll let you know when I'm finished." She grinned and went back to slowly sipping the water.

"Hey!" He nudged her in the side with his body. Ana held her ground and kept drinking. "Come on, I'm dying here!" She knew he was teasing and enjoyed it. Her mother told her that boys act like this with girls when they secretly like them. Ana grinned without lifting her head.

Well, I guess Carter Hudson has his secrets, too.

She finished, stepped to the side and pointed at the water fountain. "There you go. I hope I left you enough to keep you alive. I sure wouldn't want you passing out right here in the hall." She licked the drops of water from her lips and then used her hands to fix her long, blonde hair. She enjoyed the fact that Carter was staring at her.

"Well, I can't think of a better place to pass out," he said, "than right here with you." She watched his face turn red. Carter quickly added, "uh...in church." He leaned over the water fountain and started drinking.

Ana blushed, too, and turned away so he wouldn't notice. "I better get to class. See you later."

Carter didn't respond but just nodded his head up and down in the arching water. Ana was glad that he hadn't mentioned what had happened the day before at the newspaper. As she walked along, she thought about it.

Maybe he doesn't know. I mean, how many kids my age really know what's going on around them? I can't believe how ignorant I used to be.

She made it to her class, just as a soft gong sounded through the halls.

"Sorry, I'm late," she offered to her teacher, Courtney Thompson, who was standing in the doorway as Ana walked past her into the room.

Her teacher smiled. "You're right on time."

Ana sat down in the last empty seat at the rectangular, wooden table. Mrs. Thompson welcomed each of the six girls. They were all about the same age as Ana, and she knew a couple of them from school. Before, the teacher had always started off by asking the girls if they wanted to share something interesting from the previous week. But since Ana had become a multi-millionaire, she figured that Mrs. Thompson knew that her "something interesting from last week" would probably out-shine anything that someone else might share. Ana was thankful that her teacher was so considerate and wise. The teacher, instead, began with what she called an "ice breaker."

"What would you do if you could be invisible for a day?" she asked.

The unexpected question caught Ana by surprise.

What would I do if I could be invisible for a day?

Without warning, the most frightening moment of her life—when Lawrence Hill had almost caught her hiding beneath Rudolph Griffin's desk—forced its way into her thoughts. She squirmed in her seat as she recalled how terrified she had been and how she had silently cried out to God for help. Ana was so seized by the dreadful memory that she was unaware of the answers her classmates were giving.

"Ana?" Mrs. Thompson's voice startled her back into the present.

"Oh! Yes, ma'am?" Ana shook her head to clear it.

"What would you do if you were invisible for a day?"

"Well, uh, I..." she stalled, struggling to come up with something, anything. "If I was invisible for a whole day, I could..." For some unknown reason, she thought of Ricky and laughed nervously. "If I was invisible, I would walk into the cage of a dangerous animal—like a tiger or a lion—and he couldn't see me."

"Ooh, yeah," agreed a couple of the girls.

"That would be awesome!" exclaimed the girl to Ana's right. "I should have thought of that!"

The last girl to speak up was Olivia Freeman, who was famous for saying out loud what everyone else was quietly thinking.

"I know exactly what I would do!" she announced. "I would stand right in the middle of the boys and listen to what they are saying about us girls!"

"Oh, yes!" they all howled. The girls on either side of Olivia patted her on the back.

Mrs. Thompson laughed, too. "Thank you, Olivia, for your entertaining answer. Now, is everyone ready to study God's Word?"

"Yes, ma'am!" they all chimed in like a girls' chorus and laughed again.

After offering a brief prayer, the teacher began. "Today, our Bible story is about Jesus and the great catch of fish. It's in the Gospel of Luke, chapter 5, verses 1-11. Like we do every time, I'm first going to tell the story. Pay close attention, because when I'm finished, we're going to take turns and see how much each of you can remember. After that, we'll read it in the Bible and see what we missed. And after that," she paused, and everyone snickered, "and after that, we'll ask our questions and see what each one of you thinks. Okay?"

"Yes, ma'am!" the girls responded. Ana leaned forward and put both elbows on the table, resting her chin in her hands. As Mrs. Thompson told the highlights of the story from memory, Ana studied every detail of her teacher's kind face.

I love her. All she cares about is making sure that we know who Jesus was and what He did for us. And what we get to do for Him! She's amazing!

Ana sat up straight in her seat and started paying attention to the story. She wanted to be ready when it was her turn to talk.

* * * * *

After Sunday School, Ana thanked her teacher and walked out of the room. Andrew was leaning against the wall on the opposite side of the hall. He stood up straight when he saw her. Ana smiled at him.

"What would you do, if you could be invisible for one day?" she asked.

"Hmm," he muttered. "That's a good one. I'll have to think about it and get back to you."

They turned and strolled down the hall toward the main worship area. Ana chuckled.

"You know, even if you were invisible, there are still a lot of places you couldn't go."

"Why is that?"

"Because you're so big!" she laughed. "You wouldn't fit."

"Like where, for instance?" He stopped and looked at her. Ana immediately thought about the secret door to the tunnel she had discovered at the creek below the wall of the Griffin Estate.

"Well there are a lot of doors you might want to walk through, but you wouldn't be able to squeeze through them."

"Oh, yeah," he said and rubbed his chin. They rounded the corner and Ana caught a glimpse of her parents in the crowded hall.

"There they are," she motioned with her head. The two of them sped up and were right behind Ana's parents as they entered the auditorium.

"Ronnie, do you see them anywhere?" she heard her mother ask.

Ana's father turned around and laughed. "Uh, yep."

"Where?"

"Right behind us."

The family found seats in the auditorium. Ana glanced around and saw that Carter Hudson and his family were seated directly behind them. The congregation stood to sing the first song. Ana whispered the words softly so that she could listen to Carter singing. She grinned.

I just love church.

Later during the service, Ana watched as the ushers began taking up the morning offering. She reached into her Bible and pulled out the envelope with her offering check inside. From the time she was old enough to receive a weekly allowance, her parents had taught her to "tithe"—to give at least ten percent. Before, she had always given one dollar, because her weekly allowance was ten dollars. Now, the offering envelope in her hand held considerably more. Ana bowed her head.

Dear God, thank You that Chuck showed me that dividend statement for $187,344 dollars and 73 cents. Please use these $18,735 dollars to grow Your kingdom. Amen.

Because her name and the amount were written on the outside of the envelope, she placed it upside down in the plate, so only she, her parents, Chuck, the church counting team, and God would know how much it was.

After the worship service, Ana and her family stood in the line of people waiting their turn to speak to the pastor.

"Thank you for the sermon today, Dr. Barnes. I got a lot out of it, because you used the same Bible verses that we had in Sunday School."

"Well, I'm glad, because that's what we hoped would happen," he chuckled. He bent down and whispered in her ear. "We've sent most of the money you've given recently to disaster relief, to help the thousands of devastated hurricane victims recover. I just wanted you to know."

"Thank you, Dr. Barnes," Ana whispered. "I know you and our church leaders will do what you think Jesus wants you to do with the money. I hope you and your family have a wonderful Sunday."

* * * * *

On their way home, the family stopped at *Tasty Chicken*. Even though Ana could now afford to dine with her family in the most expensive restaurant on the planet, she still enjoyed the taste of *fast food*. And *Tasty Chicken* was hard to beat. Pulling around to the drive-thru, her father placed their usual order.

"Anything else?" asked the crackling voice on the other end.

"Oh yes," he added, "we need an extra order of biscuits please." Ana smiled because she saw her brother lean up right behind her father's head.

"With extra honey!" yelled Connor, and everyone laughed.

Chapter Five

After Sunday dinner, Ana helped clean up. Her mother spooned the precious leftover mashed potatoes and Cole slaw into plastic containers. The biscuits, of course, were all gone. Her father was in the living room, lying on the couch, watching a sports show on TV.

"Mom?" The tone of Ana's voice sounded like a question. "I need Andrew to take me to the estate this afternoon, if that's okay. I want to see what the lawn service got done yesterday," she paused, "and I need to check on something in the mansion."

Her mother smiled at her. "Thank you for asking permission, Ana. We are so proud of you and trust you completely to do what you think you need to do when and how you think you need to do it." She laughed. "Did that make any sense to you?"

"Yes, ma'am." Ana hugged her. "We'll be back before dinner."

"I want to go!" demanded Connor from behind the door, where he had been hiding. Ana glanced toward her mother and slightly shook her eyes and head back and forth. Nancy Stilwell understood the gesture. She turned toward Ana's younger brother and held up her hand like a stop sign.

"No, Connor. Not this time. Ana doesn't need you bothering her," she instructed. Ana left her mother to deal with her brother's begging, strolled out of the kitchen, and began climbing the stairs. She could overhear Connor making his case and paused to listen.

"But Andrew's going with her! I'll just stay with him. I promise not to bug her! Honest! Please, make her let me go! Please?"

"No, Connor. Not this time," her mother held firm. Ana took a deep breath.

Thanks, Mom.

* * * * *

Minutes later, she and Andrew were gliding down Griffin Avenue. When they came to the huge wrought iron gate of the main entrance, Andrew slowed down. Ana cried out, "Oh, wow! It's all cleaned up!" Andrew didn't respond but kept driving. Upon arrival at the rear service entrance, he entered the security code. Ana sat quietly as the solid wooden barrier slowly yawned open in front of them. On the other side, Andrew tapped in the code to close the gate behind them.

"Let me make sure it's locked." He turned off the car and hopped out. Even though Ana was used to the drill, she watched her bodyguard through the rear window.

You're not taking any chances, are you?

"They've been working here, too," Andrew calmly noted as he cranked the car. He drove slowly, so Ana could enjoy the view.

"I love it!" she exclaimed. "They're doing such a good job! It's beginning to look so much better. I'm really glad we hired these guys."

Andrew guided the Mercedes around the wide circular parking area in front of the mansion's main entrance. "Wow!" exclaimed Ana as she saw the fountain finally cleared of debris. "I can't wait for summer to get here so that we can turn on the water!"

"Well, they will need to pressure wash it first and check the water lines," he explained. "It'll be a miracle if the pump still works." Ana glanced over at him and then back at the fountain.

"There's still so much to do outside and inside," she stated softly, "and it's going to take a lot of time." After a brief pause, she continued, but now with a very determined tone in her voice. "But I'm going to get it all done, and I'm going to make sure that everything's done right."

"Oh, I don't have any doubt about that," muttered Andrew under his breath.

They got out and walked up the steps onto the spacious covered entryway. Ana watched as Andrew pulled out the key and unlocked the magnificent front door. Since inheriting Griffin's fortune, Ana had been so busy with settling the will, going to all kinds of meetings, setting up her foundations with mountains of paperwork, and last, but not least, buying the local newspaper, that cleaning the inside of the mansion had been put on hold. The grand dining hall had been fixed up for her recent twelfth birthday, but otherwise, everything looked like it did on the day she found the will. They entered the main entrance hall and Andrew closed the door behind them. "Please wait right here," he instructed, "while I clear the bottom floor and make sure no one is in here with us." He glanced at Ana. "Do you have your whistle?"

"Right here!" She held it up in front of her. "See? Do you want me to blow it to make sure it works?"

"No. I'm sure it works. I just wanted to make sure you didn't leave it at home like last time," he frowned. "That whistle not only lets me know you're in trouble, but it could also startle your attacker and give you a chance to run away."

"Why don't you give me a small can of pepper spray, too? That way I could nail them in the face and then blow the whistle," Ana smirked.

"You watch way too many movies," Andrew shook his head. "I'll be right back."

She didn't respond, hoping that he would get on with it. Ana watched as he quickly checked the huge main entrance hall and then disappeared down one of the side corridors.

Hurry up, please. There's something I've got to do, too.

In the process of finding the lost will, Ana had entered the mansion through a masterfully concealed paneled door in one of the rear hallways. She had always been careful to leave it standing slightly open while she was inside and had been careful to shut it tightly behind her each time she left. But she had never had to find the completely closed secret door and wasn't sure she could find it again.

It's the only way to get down into the tunnels— especially the one that's sealed off by that

*metal plate. I can't get in through the hidden
entrance at the creek because Andrew almost
never lets me out of his sight anymore.*

She paused and strained to hear her
bodyguard's footsteps.

*And I can't go through Ricky's underground
house beneath the orchard, because the gate in
the tunnel is shut tight—there's no way I can
get through it from this side. So...*

She let out a deep sigh.

*...I've got to find the hidden door in the
hallway!*

Andrew suddenly appeared. "All clear down
here," he announced and headed straight
toward her but didn't stop. Instead, he walked
past her to the front door. "I'll be back when
I'm finished with my rounds outside." He
opened the door and looked at his watch. "It's
almost 3:30 p.m. now. I should be back in,
say, twenty-five minutes."

"No problem," replied Ana. "I'll be fine." She
rolled her eyes at him.

"If you need me, call me on your cell phone
and I'll come running. Okay? Do you have your
phone?"

"Yes!" Ana pulled out her phone and held it up. "I've got my cell phone. It's got almost a full charge, and I've got you on speed dial." She jammed the phone back in her pocket and held up her whistle. "And I have my trusty whistle right here."

Andrew didn't pick up on the sarcastic tone of her voice. "When I get back," he said, "I'll knock three times to let you know it's me. Okay?"

"Sounds like a plan," she responded.

"That's what you say every time when I give you security instructions."

"Really?" she glared at him. "I wasn't aware of that."

"Ugh!" he groaned and walked through the door. Ana closed it behind him and locked it. She heard him jiggle the door latch to make sure. "See you in about twenty-five minutes," he called.

"I'll be fine!" Ana yelled and watched through the intricately carved crystal glass as his huge form faded away.

Don't worry about me, Mr. Andrew Collins. I've been in here all by myself before.

Ana patted her pocket and felt the outline of the skeleton key.

I know what I'm doing.

She spun around and took off almost running. She made her way across the magnificent room, down the long-carpeted side corridor and stopped where it joined the rear cross-hallway of the mansion. Nothing had changed. She let her gaze wander down the black and white tiled floor, framed by gorgeous paneled walls, still covered with dust and cobwebs and tracks.

Huh? Why didn't I notice that before?

The paneled wall on the right side of the hall was broken up by several closed doors.

There are rooms on the same side as the secret passageway! Oh, my goodness. I guess I was so scared that I just ignored them.

Ana opened the first door. Wooden chairs were arranged around a table. On the right side of the room was a long kitchen counter with a sink, some shelves, and a microwave. A television was on a table in the corner.

This must have been a break room for the staff.

Ana shut the door and walked down the hall to the next door. It was a storage room. The tracks and mess on the floor told her that Lawrence Hill had searched it. Plastic bottles and jugs of different shapes and sizes lay scattered. Built-in cabinets from the floor to the ceiling lined both walls on the right and left of the room. At the back were shelves with vases, bowls, and other long-ignored table decorations. There was no window. On the floor were several small, opened boxes, that Ana supposed had once also been on the shelves. She opened the closest cabinet on the wall to her right.

"Bed linens and pillowcases," she muttered. It was obvious that Hill had frantically searched here, too. Ana stuck her hand in between the sheets on one of the shelves. "Ooh! Wow! These are super soft!" she exclaimed. She opened the next cabinet. It was full of fluffy towels arranged on the shelves by color and size. She opened the next one. "More towels!" she cried. "Mom will love this! We won't ever need to buy another towel or sheet for the rest of our lives." She walked to the opposite side of the room and grabbed the knob of another cabinet but then let it go.

What am I doing? I don't have time to waste. I've got to find the secret door before Andrew gets back!

Pulling out her cell phone, she checked the time.

"Move it, girl!" she fussed. "You've got to find that door!"

Hurrying back out into the hall, she gazed up and down. Ana had done such a good job of not disturbing the cobwebs and dust before, that she now had no idea of exactly where to look. She felt sure, however, it had to be somewhere past the second door; but where? She noticed the design of the panels on the walls. Each section appeared to be about two feet wide. She began pushing on them, but nothing budged.

This is crazy! I know it's here. It's got to be here!

Ana stepped back and studied the wall directly in front of her.

"Calm down!" she commanded. "Let's start again and do this systematically." Ana walked back down to the panel next to the storage room door and pushed on the wall. Then it hit her.

What am I doing? Duh! I don't need to push. I need to pull on them! The secret door opens out into the hall! What a goofball I am!

She moved back to where she figured the hidden door should be.

Okay. From inside the secret passageway the door was hinged on the right, so that means it opens out and to the left. I need to pull on the right side of the panel to open it.

Ana firmly gripped the trim with both hands and yanked. Without a sound, the secret door popped open.

"Yes!" Her cry echoed down the empty halls. She shushed herself, like so many times before, but then burst out laughing, "Why do I need to be quiet?" Ana shouted. "Hello? I don't have to worry about Lawrence Hill or anybody else! This place belongs to me!" Ana knew she was being silly but didn't care.

The secret hallway behind the door was pitch black, but Ana knew where she was. She clicked on her flashlight, stepped from the tracks in the dust onto the stone floor of the

67

hidden passageway and walked to the top of the stairs. Directing the light downward, she could make out the wooden door at the bottom. It was still closed and locked—just like she had left it. Ana pulled out the skeleton key and turned it over in her hand.

I don't have time today, but at least I know now that I can get back down into the tunnels whenever I need to.

Ana jammed the key back in her pocket and retraced her steps. Back out in the rear hallway of the mansion, she quietly pushed the hidden paneled door shut.

Ana noticed the small smudges left by her fingerprints.

"Uh, oh. I better get rid of these!"

After finishing, she stepped back to examine the results and thought about Rudolph Griffin.

I'm sure you never had to worry about dust and fixing cobwebs.

"But, hey! At least I found your hidden door again," she listened to her words echo through the halls and laughed out loud. "Uh, my hidden door!" Ana checked the time on her cell phone.

Andrew will be back soon.

Once again in the main entrance hall, she stood there gazing at the wondrous sight and remembered the way she felt the first time she had seen it. Bending over backwards, she looked upward toward the second and third-floor balconies.

I really need to check out those floors. If he took the time to build a hidden passageway and dig secret tunnels, what else am I going to find... up there?

Ana gazed upward at the vaulted ceiling.

Bam! Bam! Bam!

She almost leaped out of her skin. "Talk about scaring me half to death!" Ana spun around and recognized Andrew's huge form through the thick glass. He was bent over, trying to look through it, while at the same time, attempting to unlock the door with his key.

"I'm coming!" she called.

Andrew opened the door. "Are you finished?"

"All finished," she replied.

...for today.

CHapter Six

"Ana? Connor? Are you up yet?" her father yelled down the hall. "Come on, you sleepy heads! It might be raining on the outside, but it's still time to rise and shine on the inside!"

Ana turned over in her bed and covered her head with the pillow. Even though she was now extremely wealthy, her parents still expected her to get up, get ready for school and get downstairs for breakfast. The soothing, rhythmic sounds of the rain on the roof above her head made her want to ignore her father's command...at least for a few more minutes. But she knew that wasn't going to happen. Even though her door was shut, she could hear him marching down the hall. He wasn't trying to be quiet. He never did.

Without warning, he pounded on her door from the other side. Ana grinned. She knew it was coming, so she wasn't startled by it at all.

"Come on, young lady! Get a move on!" She mouthed the words as he shouted them through the door. Ana didn't respond. She heard him walk across the hall and beat on her brother's door, open it, enter his room and lovingly demand, "Come on, Master Stilwell, rise and shine!" Ana knew that wouldn't be enough to budge him—not on a rainy Monday morning. Connor would burrow deeper in the covers like a prairie dog. Her dad would have to catch him, drag him out of bed and ignore his protests. Ana put her hands behind her head and listened to the commotion going on. Her brother, who never wanted to go to bed at night, now complained that he was too tired to get up.

It was early March but still dark outside. Ana watched the shadows dancing on her ceiling made by the streetlight in front of their house shining through the moving tree branches and smiled.

I think dad loves it when we don't get up on time. He enjoys yelling the same old thing, coming up here, banging on our doors and doing battle with Connor.

Ana snuggled under her own covers for the few remaining, precious seconds, waiting for the inevitable final pounding. Her door shook again.

"I'm up! I'm up!" she called. Ana took a deep breath and let it out.

Thanks, Dad for staying just the way you are.

On this rainy Monday morning, Ana and Connor didn't slog their way to school in their raincoats like they had done so many times before. Andrew drove them. Not because it was raining, but because now he drove Ana almost every place she went—in one of her ridiculously valuable, vintage Mercedes that she had inherited from the Griffin Estate.

When Chuck had explained to her that it would reduce their value to drive them, Ana had replied, "There is no need to go buy another car for Andrew to haul me around in, since I already own three. If they run, let's use them."

Connor, of course, loved being driven to school every day. He waved out the window to Johnny Ralston and the other students making their way down the sidewalk as they passed by. As always, he begged Andrew to honk the horn, but that didn't happen.

The rain began to let up as they arrived at Lewistowne South Elementary School. Ana was still in the sixth grade. She and her family had only lived in Lewistowne since the previous summer.

Back then, Ana had a difficult time adjusting to school. She wasn't that shy but had been totally brand new, and Skylar Perkins, *the queen of the sixth grade*, had not helped the situation. The day after Ana had told her that she was going to check out the town's library— Ana found out later—Skylar had immediately begun telling the other girls that she was "a major, stuck-up, know-it-all weirdo." Ana never got used to Skylar and her gang staring, pointing, whispering, and laughing at her. Skylar was the reason that Ana had been doomed to sit alone in the lunchroom every day.

Now she was sitting all by herself again. And Skylar and her bunch were still staring and whispering about her.

Looks like being a millionaire doesn't mean much to girls my age. They are still as nasty as ever. I think I'm going to start praying for them. Lord knows, they need it.

Andrew was sitting in a chair in the corner of the lunchroom watching the door. Ana saw Skylar point at him and say something. The girls around her broke into wicked laughter. Ana looked down at her plate and went back to eating. Suddenly the room fell silent, causing her to glance over toward Skylar's table.

I wonder what shut them up.

Unknown to Ana, a boy had entered the lunchroom near the serving line. He was holding his tray and was making his way from behind Ana straight to where she was sitting. Ana didn't see him, but she did see the expression on Skylar Perkins' face change from one of devilish glee to like she had just bitten into a rotten tomato.

"Hey there, rich girl!" Carter Hudson joked as he plopped down his tray and sat in the seat across the table from her.

"Please don't call me that," frowned Ana, "It's bad enough that I have to be protected every second of the day. You don't know what my life is like now. It's not as easy as you think."

"I'm sorry, I was just kidding."

Ana grinned at him. "That's okay, but I guess you are right, though."

"What do you mean?"

"I am a rich girl." She glanced down at her plate and moved the food around with her fork.

"Just how rich are you?" he blurted out before thinking. Carter apologized immediately. "Ana, I'm sorry. That's none of my business."

She took a drink of water and shook her head. "Don't worry about it. Truth is, I don't really know myself... not exactly." She looked up at him. "But it is an awful lot. Do you promise not to tell anyone?"

Carter leaned across the table and looked her straight in the eyes, "I will die before I tell anyone. I promise." Ana studied the contours of his face and smiled as sweetly as she could—loving every second of it. She glanced over at Skylar Perkins, who was not loving every second of it. She looked back at Carter.

"At the last count, I'm worth over two hundred fifty million dollars." His mouth dropped open and her smile vanished. She was wondering how he would react. Carter closed his eyes and bowed his head. Ana enjoyed the details of his blonde hair. She wondered if he might be praying. But then he let out a groan, lifted his head and stared at her.

"Good night! Are you serious?"

"Uh, huh," she nodded slightly, "and it is growing more and more every day. Mr. Switcher is always finding money, stuff and companies that I own."

"Like the newspaper?"

She blushed. "I wondered if you were going to say something about that." Ana knew that

Carter enjoyed teasing her and didn't draw back as he leaned in close to her again.

"I would have loved to have seen the face of Winton Pressley when it happened," he whispered. "My uncle works at the place and told us yesterday afternoon about your speech. He is so excited that he's going to get to work for you, instead of old Pressley. He said that you really care about people... that people trust you."

Ana watched Carter's face. She was so thankful that at least one of her classmates still talked to her like a normal person. And she was extra thankful it was him. She glanced across the room. Skylar Perkins and her mob were glaring at her.

* * * * *

That afternoon Ana quickly finished her homework and looked out the window.

Oh, good. It's stopped raining.

She changed out of her school clothes into a pair of jeans and her favorite pink sweatshirt. Not knowing where Connor might be lurking, she crept down the hall and began tiptoeing down the stairs.

Andrew had stationed himself in the living room where he could monitor the staircase and saw her coming. Connor was sitting on the floor just a few feet away, twitching and turning and fussing at the television screen— seriously involved in one of his XBOX games. Ana could hear her younger brother as she made her way down the steps.

As soon as she made eye contact with her bodyguard, she waved her hand back and forth and up and down in front of her face, signaling to him to be quiet and to not stand up. Andrew grinned, nodded, and motioned toward Connor. Ana put her finger across her lips, giving him the "please be quiet" sign. Andrew responded with a "thumbs up". She stopped at the bottom of the stairs and motioned for him to join her in the hallway.

"Go! Go! Go!" screamed Connor—his eyes glued to the action in front of him. Andrew got up and inched slowly out of the room.

Out of the corner of her eye, Ana saw her mother moving about in the kitchen. She walked to the door. There were papers and glue and an assortment of craft items lying on the table. Ana smiled. Her mother enjoyed making family scrap books, and since Ana's new-found fame, had plenty of new items to add.

"Mom?" she whispered. Her mother was walking across the room with a pair of scissors and spun around. She had obviously heard her daughter's whisper and responded with one.

"What?" she said softly, laid the scissors on the table and moved toward her daughter. Just then Connor let out a yell of delight from the living room. "What's up?"

"I need Andrew to drive me over to the mansion again. I just wanted you to know where we are."

"How long will you be gone?" her mother asked.

"Not long." The odd look on Ana's face must have let her mother know that this was serious.

"Is there anything wrong?" she inquired.

"No ma'am." Ana stared at her mother, tip-toed up and whispered in her ear. "I want Andrew to help me check on the condition of the Griffin family graves. I need to see inside the mausoleum."

"Oh, Ana!" Her mother recoiled and glared at her daughter.

"Mom... it's my responsibility," she stated firmly. "I need to do this."

Nancy Stilwell's expression changed instantly from one of shock to admiration. She leaned over and hugged her daughter. "I know. I know," she sighed. "Just be careful."

"I will," promised Ana. She turned and saw Andrew standing in the doorway to the kitchen. She walked over to him and whispered in his ear. "I need you to take me to the mansion, and I don't want Connor to know." She and Andrew crept down the hall, past the living room, and slowly opened the front door.

Squeak! The hinges screeched, echoing through the house. They both cringed and peered back toward the living room. Ana knew her brother had excellent hearing and expected him to come sliding out into the hall. Seconds passed.

"Oh baby! Go! Go! Go!" she heard him scream at his digital Formula 1 race car. Ana looked up at Andrew.

"Thank goodness, he's in his own little world."

"Yep." Andrew followed her out the door. "What's up? Why do we need to go to the mansion?"

Ana bit her lower lip and took a deep breath. "I need you to help me do something that I can't do... that I don't want to do by myself."

"What's that?"

"I need you to open the door to the mausoleum where the Griffins are buried. I've never been in there and I want to see what it looks like inside."

"Oh," shuddered Andrew. "Do we have to do it today?"

"If you don't mind," she studied the expression on his face and teased, "you're not scared, are you?"

"Me?" Andrew stood up straight and gazed over her head, looking around like he was checking the area for threats. "No. Of course not."

Ana snickered, "Well, I'm glad to hear it, because I wouldn't want to ask you do something that might give you the *heebie-jeebies*." The two of them walked toward her Mercedes.

"I don't get the *heebie-jeebies*," he said flatly and opened the door for her to get in. He walked around the car and Ana watched him get in on the driver's side.

No. You're right. You give other people the heebie-jeebies.

CHapter Seven

When they arrived at the estate, the service gate was standing wide open.

"Well, that's not good," Andrew complained, as they drove through. "Must be the lawn service guys. I can't believe they didn't close it." She watched as he got out and made sure the gate was shut. She noticed the scowl on his face as he got back into the car.

They drove along and Ana spied the lawn service truck and trailer. She undid her seatbelt, leaned forward, and pointed across Andrew's chest out the window to the left. "There they are on the other side of the tennis courts." Andrew glared at her and then down at her unfastened seat belt. Ana knew immediately that she had messed up. "Sorry." She quickly buckled her seatbelt across her lap and chest.

"Please never forget," he explained, "that my main job is to keep you safe at all times... no matter what."

"I know," sighed Ana. Her parents and Chuck had explained to her why they had hired Andrew—why she needed a bodyguard. She wondered if she would need one for the rest of her life. Ana gazed out the window.

Before I got so rich, nobody, other than mom or dad—and Jesus—cared about where I was or what I was doing. Nobody was worried about somebody kidnapping me to hold me for ransom. Life sure was easier—back when I was poor.

The Mercedes rolled to a stop in the parking lot toward the rear of the mansion. Ana looked up at it.

Well, I'm just going to have to get used to it. Anyway, I'm glad I found the will and not old Lawrence Hill. He would have probably moved in here and acted like he was the King of the World.

Ana got out of the car and saw where the lawn crew had been busy trimming with their weed-eaters. "I love it," she said happily. She joined Andrew at the edge of the parking lot. In front of them was a path, approximately three feet wide, but still almost completely overgrown with grass and weeds. Ana could tell that it was made of small, white rocks. The two of them followed the path around the rear of the mansion to wide stone steps that led up to the side of the very large, raised terrace. Wrought iron chairs were arranged in conversation groups. Other tables and chairs were placed for dinners and entertaining. Ana saw several large, bleached-out umbrellas standing folded up like silent sentries in their rusted stands. She walked over and touched the back of the chair closest to her.

I wonder what it looked like when they had parties and music and famous guests wandering around, laughing, and having fun?

Andrew stood quietly. Ana glanced over at him but didn't say anything. Over his right shoulder she glimpsed the mausoleum in the distance.

"You ready?"

"Yes, ma'am, whenever you are."

She led the way down the steps and along the path toward the tomb.

"He had this built for his wife, Beatrice," she explained as they walked along. Andrew followed closely behind her until she stopped directly in front of the imposing structure. "It's made of marble that he had shipped over from Carrera, Italy."

"Wow," uttered Andrew. "I wonder how much *that* cost?"

"He didn't care." Ana walked up and rested her right hand gently on one of the cold columns. "She had cancer. He was so rich, but he couldn't keep her from dying."

Andrew didn't respond.

In front of them stood the massive copper door that had turned dark green from years of neglect. "I can't wait to have this cleaned," stated Ana as she rubbed her hand across the *bas-relief* carvings on the front. She looked at Andrew with a stern expression on her face. "I want this place to shine! I want it to look like it did on the day he buried her." Ana moved to the side and he stepped forward.

"It looks like all I have to do is turn this handle," he explained. "I don't think its locked." She watched him grab the long, metal latch with both hands, turn it up and to the left. The deep metal scraping sound of the bolt sliding sent a chill up and down Ana's back.

There's no way I could have done this by myself.

Andrew strained to force open the heavy door. The crusted hinges groaned as if they didn't want to be disturbed.

It's like Indiana Jones in one of his movies, opening some ancient, mysterious crypt.

Ana followed her bodyguard through the door. Once inside, they both waited for their eyes to adjust to the darkness.

"Oh wow!" they cried in unison. The light pouring in through the intricate, leaded-crystal windows, cast wondrous patterns of color everywhere. They both stood completely still, trying to take it all in.

"It is so beautiful in here," Ana said in a hushed, reverent tone. "Even on a dreary day like this, it's magnificent." Detailed carvings of angels, vines, and flowers graced the marble walls, framed by the delicate curves of gothic-shaped columns. Three raised, white marble tombs, with exquisitely carved floral designs, stood in the middle of the room.

The one in the center had "My darling, Beatrice" engraved on one end. Lewis's tomb was the closest to Ana and Andrew. On the other side of Beatrice's tomb was Rudolph Griffin's. A large, heavy-looking, hand-cut crystal vase adorned the top of each grave. All three vases were identical...almost.

"Look, this one had flowers in it," said Ana and pointed at the one on Beatrice's grave. The crumbled, dusty remains of what was once a floral bouquet partially filled the vase. The rest littered the top of the tomb. She gestured toward Lewis' grave. "His vase had flowers in it, too."

"But," Andrew pointed, "the vase on Mr. Griffin's tomb looks completely empty."

"You know what I think?" she pursed her lips. "Rudolph Griffin always made sure that fresh flowers were on their graves, but when he died, there was nobody left to put flowers on his. I'll bet you no one has been in here since he was buried." Her remark made her think about Lawrence Hill.

I wonder if you thought about coming out here and searching for the will?

"There's a sink over there with a faucet." Ana turned to see where Andrew was pointing. It was beautifully carved and inset into a sculpted corner of the room.

"What a great idea!" she approved. "Would you see if the water works?"

"Sure," Andrew walked over and turned on the faucet. The lively noise of the steady stream echoed against the walls of the mausoleum.

"I'm going to make sure that they always have fresh flowers on their graves," she declared. Ana glanced back at the crystal vase on Lewis' tomb and motioned with her hand. "Let's rinse them out so we won't have to when we come back with the flowers."

"Good idea," agreed Andrew.

"Let's do Lewis' vase first," she suggested.

"This thing is heavy," he said as he lifted it off the tomb. As he turned around toward her, Ana noticed something stuck to the base of the vase.

"What's that?" she pointed.

"It looks like some kind of sticker." Andrew tilted it over so Ana could see the small, silver-edged label.

Blei-Krystall aus Bayern

"I can't make out what it says. It's not written in English."

Andrew held the vase so he could see it. "I think it might be German."

"If it is German," Ana pulled out her cell phone and tapped on the camera app, "I can ask Ms. Quillian my history teacher. She spent a whole month in Germany when she was 28 years old. I'll bet she'll know what it says."

"How old is she now?" inquired Andrew.

"Calm down," Ana winked. "She's too old for you." She motioned with her hand. "Would you please lift up the bottom of the vase so I can see the label?" She moved in closer. "Hold it steady," she instructed and took the shot. Andrew lowered the vase. "Can you hold it back up again, please? I want to make another one."

Andrew let out a sigh and held it up again. Ana made another photo. "How's that one?" he groaned. She could tell he wanted this ordeal to end and checked it to make sure the words on the label were readable.

"Perfect!" Ana smiled. He lowered the heavy vase and started to set it down. "Uh, hold it up again, please. I want to get one of the whole thing." Andrew muttered something unintelligible under his breath. "Just think of it as a workout," she teased as she took a step backwards.

"Very funny," Andrew huffed and held the enormous vase out in front of him. "Please, don't get me in the photo."

"I won't." Ana adjusted her stance. "Hold it... got it!"

"Finally," he exhaled, lowered the vase and walked over to the sink. Ana turned and began lightly blowing off the dusty remains of the flowers from the top of Lewis' tomb. She did the same for Beatrice's. Before long, all three vases were back in place. The two of them stood there, proud of their accomplishment.

"I don't know if you could have done all of this by yourself," remarked Andrew.

Ana turned and glared up at him. "Well, of course, I couldn't have done this all by myself. I can't even get the door open by myself. Duh!" She shoved him as hard as she could on his upper right arm. He didn't budge at all.

"Duh?" joked Andrew grinning.

"Duh!" blurted Ana, but then stopped playing and cleared her throat. "We shouldn't be acting up like this in here," she confessed, "it's a tomb!" The smile from Andrew's face vanished. "Come on, let's go," she said and headed toward the door.

As they strolled back toward the mansion, instead of taking the walkway, they cut straight across the lawn area. The grass was in bad shape with several empty patches. In one of the larger, muddy spots, Ana recognized some familiar tracks and pointed at them.

"Ricky!"

"It sure looks like it."

She quickly glanced around in every direction. Even though the tracks looked fresh, Ana couldn't locate her pet's huge, rounded shell.

"Do you see him anywhere?"

"No, ma'am."

The voice of one of the lawn service guys hollering a command to the crew, caused her to look in the direction of the tennis courts. A very light, misty rain began to fall. Ana wondered if they had already encountered the enormous ancient reptile.

"Andrew," she said motioning in their direction, "they need to know that Ricky's crawling around in here somewhere. Please ask them to watch out for him and to not bother him."

"Will do," he replied. A chainsaw cranked up and he stared in the direction of the noise. "I also need to instruct them to text me every time before they come and when they leave." He glanced back at Ana, "and to keep the gates closed and locked at all times. We don't need your pet crawling out into traffic."

"No kidding!" she cried.

"I have their number and could phone them, but I need to give them this message in person, if you know what I mean?" Andrew was not grinning as he turned to walk away.

"Be nice," she called. "Remember that you look really scary to people who don't know you."

"Yes, ma'am," he glanced back at her and smirked. The sound of the chainsaw suddenly made her think of the orchard and the entrance to Ricky's underground home.

"And Andrew!" she yelled as loudly as she could. He stopped and turned to look at her.

"Yes, ma'am?"

"Tell them to leave the orchard and the area on the other side of the mansion completely alone! I have special plans for it." The expression on Andrew's face signaled to her that he wanted to ask *Why?* But he didn't.

"Yes, ma'am!" he saluted and jogged toward the tennis courts and the renewed whirring sound of several leaf blowers.

I don't need them finding Ricky's trap door.

* * * * *

That evening Ana called Chuck.

"Yes, ma'am?" he answered. "What can I do for you?"

"I want to put flowers—very nice flowers—on the Griffin's tombs," she explained. "Andrew and I were in the mausoleum this afternoon, and there are very large, heavy crystal vases on the tops of their graves."

"What do they look like?" he asked and added, "and how many are there?"

"Three. One on each tomb. I took a photo of Andrew holding one up so you can see how big it is," she said. "I'll text it to you."

"That'll work," he said. "Which florist do you want to use?"

"Who do you suggest?"

"I think Rachel Bennett is the best in town."

"She'll be fine," agreed Ana. "I want really nice, fresh flowers. Maybe roses. And I want red, white, and blue ribbons with their names on them."

"How much do you want to spend?" he asked. "A very nice arrangement should run between one hundred and two hundred dollars."

"Let's go with two hundred dollars for each one," she instructed.

"Yes, ma'am," Chuck noted. "When do you want to pick them up?"

Ana thought a minute. "How about on Friday afternoon after school?"

"Friday afternoon, every other week. Are you sure?"

"Sounds good to me," approved Ana.

"When do you want to start?" he asked.

"If possible, I'd like to start this Friday," she said hopefully.

"I'll be sure to carefully spell out each name for her," stated Chuck, "and I'll ask her to box them up for transport, and," Ana could tell he was making notes, "I'll get her to mail the invoice to me, so you won't have to worry about paying for them."

"Thank you so much," said Ana gratefully.

"You are very welcome, Miss Stilwell."

Chapter Eight

Skylar Perkins was waiting on Ana when she walked in the school's main entrance the next morning. The expression on her face was one that Ana had never seen before.

What is this all about? Has she been crying?

"Ana, can I talk to you?" Skylar glared at Andrew and then back at Ana, "in private?"

"Sure. I guess so." Ana twisted around, held up her hand and whispered, "Can we have a little space?" Andrew moved back several steps and crossed his arms. Ana had told him about the *queen of the sixth grade,* and she had seen this same exact expression on his face before. It always meant: *'Do you really want to do this?'* She nodded at him and mouthed silently: *'It's okay.'* Ana turned back around and watched her classmate wipe her eyes and nose on her sleeve. "What's happened? What's got you so upset?"

"My father lost his job two weeks ago!" Her voice was quivering. "It came as a complete shock. I overhead him and mom talking last night. He didn't do anything wrong. Some bigger bank bought out the bank where he worked. Dad said he was a 'victim of downsizing'—whatever that means. My mom was crying. They're scared. I'm scared," she sniffed and continued, "and he told her that we won't be able to make this month's house payment." She stared at Ana and then dropped her head, sobbing. "He said all of our savings, all of our money is gone." Her shoulders were shaking.

As Ana listened, she thought about all the mean things that Skylar had done to her and all the rumors she had spread about her behind her back. She wanted to snatch her by the nose and scream, "Well, it serves you right, you demon!" But then Ana remembered that Jesus—somewhere in the Bible—said we need to love our enemies and do good to those who persecute us! Ana sighed deeply and closed her eyes.

Lord Jesus, I can't believe I am asking this, but please help me to love Skylar Perkins like You do. Amen.

She reached out to put her arm around Skylar, and her sworn enemy melted into her embrace. Peeking over her shoulder, Ana saw Andrew make a move toward the two of them, probably to free her from Skylar's grasp, so she shook her head at him. Ana had never been this close to Skylar Perkins... ever.

Talk about miracles! I'm actually hugging the absolutely most stuck up and nastiest girl in the whole school. Only Jesus could do this.

"Skylar, is there anything I can do?"

Skylar sniffed, "Well, I hate to ask you, but one of the girls told me yesterday that you bought the newspaper. Do you...do you think you might have a job for my dad?" she started sobbing again. Ana could tell her fear was genuine and felt sorry for her. Then Skylar said something that caught Ana by surprise. "I wouldn't blame you, if you don't want to help him, uh, us," she paused and hung her head again, "because of the horrible way I've treated you since you moved here. Please forgive me, Ana." Holding her classmate in her arms, Ana gazed up at the ceiling and closed her eyes in prayer again.

Dear Lord Jesus, please let there be a job for Skylar's dad at my newspaper. Amen.

She pushed Skylar up and held her by the shoulders. "Listen to me," she stared directly into her red, puffy, soggy face. "I forgive you."

"Are you serious?" her classmate blurted out.

"Yes, of course." Ana pulled her close to her, so that the other students walking past couldn't hear. "Tell your dad to go by the newspaper and apply for a job. I'll call them and let them know he's coming."

"Oh, my gosh!" bawled Skylar, wiping her eyes with both hands. "That's crazy! How can you forgive me? How can you be so nice to me and my family after what I've done to you?"

"Well, I guess it's what Jesus would want me to do," she forced a smile. "Now, don't worry. I'll do what I can to help your dad find a job." She leaned in and whispered in Skylar's ear, "But please don't tell anyone about this, okay? It'll be our secret."

Skylar grabbed Ana and hugged her as tightly as she could. "Thank you! Thank you, Ana! Thank you so much!"

Ana smiled. "You're welcome. Now, go to the restroom and wash your face, so no one will know you've been crying. Come on, let's go or we'll be late for class."

"God bless you, Ana Stilwell!" Ana watched her former enemy lower her head and hurry away toward the restroom. Ana sighed.

He already has.

* * * * *

When the last bell rang, Ana didn't hurry toward the front door like she normally did but headed down the hall toward the room where she hoped to find her history teacher, Ms. Quillian. Ana had informed Andrew of her plans, so he wouldn't worry about her. She didn't worry about Connor, because she knew he would be sitting in the Mercedes like the crown prince of Lewistowne waving to his passing subjects.

"Ms. Quillian?" she called as she entered the classroom. Her teacher was not at her desk.

"Back here," came the familiar voice from behind a long cabinet door in the rear of the room. Ana walked through the rows of desks in her direction. The 65-year-old history teacher poked her head out from around the door. "Oh, hey, Ana. I thought that was you. What's up?"

"I need to show you something I found, Ms. Quillian," she said, pulling out her cell phone. "It's a sticker on the bottom of a crystal vase. I think the words might be German." Ms. Quillian shut the cabinet door and put on her glasses that had been dangling from a dark cord around her neck. Ana showed her the photo of the label.

"Blei-Krystall aus Bayern?" she read out loud. "Oh, yes. That's German all right. It means *leaded crystal from Bavaria.*"

"Where's Bavaria?" asked Ana.

"It's a large state in the southeastern part of Germany," she removed her glasses and let them hang in front of her again. Then she bent over and smiled directly at Ana. "It's where the Eagles Nest is, remember?"

"Oh yes!" cried Ana. "That place you hiked up to in the mountains. Hitler's mountain house."

"Very good" praised Ms. Quillian. "Come. Let me show you on the map where I think your vase was made." Ana followed her back to the front of the classroom. She watched as her teacher reached up to the map rolls and pulled down a detailed map of Germany over the map of Europe. "This area along the upper eastern side of Bavaria," Ana saw her wipe her finger back and forth across the map. "This is the Bavarian Forest," she turned and gazed deep into Ana's eyes. "It's where they make beautiful hand-blown, hand-cut, leaded-crystal vases, goblets, glasses, bowls, and many other amazing things. I know. I went there and watched them do it."

"You saw them making crystal vases?" exclaimed Ana and sat down in an empty desk in the front row.

"Oh, yes," beamed Ms. Quillian. She stood up straight and began moving her hands through the air like she was directing an orchestra. "They use long, hollow pipes to remove globs of glowing crystal out of red-hot furnaces, and then they swing them around and blow in them, constantly spinning the growing creation with their hands." Ana's mouth fell open in awe. She had no idea that her ancient history teacher could be so... animated.

"Wow!" muttered Ana. Ms. Quillian must have realized the scene she was making and let her arms drop.

"They create masterpieces. It's quite thrilling." She pointed back at the Bavarian Forest on the map. "So, the vase probably came from this area." She turned and looked at Ana. "I'd love to see it."

"I have a picture of it!" Ana stood up and scrolled in her phone to the photo of the vase. "See?"

"Oh, my! That is something!" Ms. Quillian instantly put her glasses back on and leaned in to get a better look. "It is expert craftmanship. Just look at the details. I'm sure it's extremely valuable. Where did you find it?"

Ana jumped like she had been hit and pulled back her phone. She saw the expression on the history teacher's face melt from excitement to extreme uneasiness. Neither of them made a sound. Seconds ticked by. Ana's former determination to keep everything about the Griffins a total secret began to be chipped away by honest considerations.

She has been so nice to help me. Why can't I tell her? It doesn't matter where I found it. Why can't she know? I might need her to help me with other things. Who knows what else I'm going to find?

"Oh, Ana. I'm so sorry. That's really none of my business, is it?" apologized Ms. Quillian.

"No. No. It's all right," she replied sweetly and gazed at her teacher's kind, wrinkled face. "I found it...on Beatrice Griffin's tomb."

The history teacher covered her mouth, "Oh, my word!"

Chapter Nine

"You were right! The words on the label are German," she announced to Andrew as she got into the car.

"Really?" He started the motor and pulled out into the traffic.

"Uh, huh. Ms. Quillian translated them, just like I thought she could." Ana glanced around at her brother in the back seat to see if he was listening. He didn't appear to be. His eyes were glued to some game on his tablet, but Ana didn't want to take any chances. Connor was a serious snoop, so he might be faking it.

"I'll tell you about it later...when it's just the two of us."

Andrew nodded but didn't say anything. The rest of the ride home was uneventful.

Later that afternoon, Ana finished her homework and looked out the window. The clouds were breaking up and the sun was shining.

What a day! I sure wish it wasn't movie night, tonight. I would love to check out the upstairs rooms in the mansion.

Ana sighed deeply.

But Mom really looks forward to making a fun dinner, popping popcorn and spending—as she puts it—quality time with us, so it'll just have to wait.

She ambled out of her room and thought about sliding down the hall in her sock feet, but even that had lost its glamour. Letting her feet slip over the edge of each step, Ana thumped her way slowly to the bottom of the stairs and sank down on the last one. Her mother heard her and walked out into the hall. Ana could tell by the unhappy look on her face that something was up.

"Ana, your father called while you were doing your homework," she explained. "A very important client from out of town needs to meet with him. It was totally unexpected and there is no way your father can put it off. He also has no idea how long the meeting will last, so we are going to have to postpone movie night."

Ana didn't look up at her mother. Instead, she covered her face with her hands.

"Don't be upset, honey." Her mother stroked her long, blonde hair. "Your father said we will just have to move movie night this week to Friday."

Her mother scratched her head. "You know, it might not be a bad idea to move movie night to Friday or even Saturday for good. I mean, that way we wouldn't have to worry about it being a school night, and if the movie is a long one, it wouldn't really matter."

Ana jumped up. "Mom! We can't move it to Saturday night because of Sunday School and church!"

"Oh, that's right!" Her mother reached over and hugged her. "Thank you so much for reminding me!" She laughed and headed toward the back of the house.

"Mom, have you seen Connor?"

Her mother turned around. "There's a new boy in his class named Stuart who invited him and Johnny Ralston over to play for a couple of hours. I let him go since movie night was called off." She disappeared through the door to the kitchen.

"Mom?" Ana called, walking toward her.

"What is it now?" she stuck her head back out into the hall.

"Since we're not having movie night, I want to ask Andrew to take me back over to the mansion? There's something I need to check on. It won't take long."

"Sure. I don't care. Stay as long as you like," her mother replied. "Just please be back in time for dinner." Andrew emerged from the kitchen with a Diet Coke in his hand and walked past Ana's mother.

"Diet Coke?" Ana pointed at the can. "Since when do you drink Diet Coke?"

"Since we are out of real Coke." He popped open the top. "What's up?"

"I need you to take me back over to the mansion, if you don't mind."

"You're the boss," he smiled and drained the can.

* * * * *

"So, what did the label on the vase say?" Andrew waited for a car to pass before he guided her Mercedes out of the driveway and onto the street.

"Oh, yeah," she turned around, wiggled in her seat excitedly, and stared at him. "Leaded crystal from Bavaria. Ms. Quillian said Bavaria is a state in southeastern Germany."

"Oh, I know where it is," he explained without taking his eyes from the road. "Bavaria, I mean. My brother's in the Army. He's just been sent to a base over there."

"Really?"

"Yes, ma'am. He hasn't traveled around much yet, but from the few photos he's put online, it looks gorgeous."

"I'd love to see them," she replied.

* * * * *

Moments later they were, once again, standing in the gorgeous entrance hall of the mansion. Ana saw Andrew glance at his watch.

"I know you need to go through your normal safety routine in here," she spoke up. "But today I would like for you to let me do something else first?"

"May I ask, what?"

"Would you mind waiting down here while I check out the upper levels? I've never been up there, and," she paused, "I want to do it today... by myself." She noticed the odd look on his face. "What is it?"

"Oh, nothing," he shook his head and began walking across the room. "May I first check out the staircase?"

106

Ana followed him. "You want to see if there are any new tracks in the dust. Right?"

Andrew turned and grinned. "You never cease to amaze me." The two of them stood staring at the trail, looking for any signs of recent activity. "Okay. Nothing new that I can see," he approved, "you are good to go. If you need me, just let me know." Ana saw him glance around and figured he was searching for a place to sit down. Nearby was an expensive-looking antique chair. He walked over to it and snorted, "There is no way that dainty thing would hold me."

"There's a nice couch in the parlor over there." She pointed back across the room at an open door to her left. "But you'll probably need to dust it off first."

"I'll be fine. Are you sure you don't want me to go with you?"

Ana glared at him, not sure how she should respond.

I needed you to help me in the mausoleum but not in here. There are things that I want to see first... to discover first. And I don't want to have to explain what I'm doing. You don't know Rudolph Griffin like I do. Nobody does. I'm not ready to reveal everything I know to anybody... not even to you. Not yet.

Andrew must have read the look on her face. Even though she was only twelve years old, she was still Ana Stilwell.

"Just let me know if you need me," he stated in a business-like manner.

She patted him on the arm, "Don't worry, I will." Ana started up the stairs and thought about Lawrence Hill.

It must be killing you to have spent so many years in here, desperately searching for the will, only to have me find it instead.

As she climbed higher and higher, she grinned.

And I didn't even have to go upstairs.

At the top, she looked back down at the main hall. There was Andrew—watching her like a hawk. Ana knew it was useless to expect him to sit down somewhere. She waved and he waved back.

"I won't be long," she called.

"Take your time."

Turning around slowly, she surveyed the second level in front of her. There were nine doors: three on her left, three on her right and three behind her. Between the doors, the walls were tastefully decorated. Large, sconce lamps that looked like golden candles separated the beautiful paintings with thick gilded frames. The wall color matched perfectly. Ana noticed the walkway balcony went all the way around the huge room. The floor was covered with the same thick carpet as some of the corridors on the first floor.

At the far end was a conversation area with high-back leather chairs and dark wooden tables. Ana's gaze continued its tour. The door to the first room to her right was standing slightly open. As she began making her way over to it, Ana noticed again the trail of tracks in the dust made by Lawrence Hill. When she reached the door, she pushed it completely open and peeked inside.

Oh, wow! What a beautiful room!

White dust covers that had once protected the bed and other expensive furniture lay crumpled in a heap on the floor. Open drawers and cabinet doors indicated that they had been searched. The shelves were in disarray and various items were scattered on the gorgeous hardwood floors. She could tell that the furniture had been shoved around. Like everywhere else in the house, the wall decorations and paintings had been pushed to the side, or completely removed and stacked against the walls. Ana disgustedly shook her head.

Did you really think he would have hidden his will behind this painting of a bunch of ducks?

She saw a door on the far side of the room.

Ooh! Ooh! Maybe, it's in there! Let's go look!

It was a large, full-size bathroom with marble-tiled walls and brass-plated fixtures.

"Oh, nice!" she gushed but then noticed that all the drawers in the vanity had been left pulled out. "Really?" Ana fumed under her breath. "You searched the guest bathroom? What a great idea! I'm sure Mr. Griffin thought about hiding the will behind the extra rolls of toilet paper."

Ana ventured from room to room on the second level. Some of them had an outside balcony, but other than that, they all were basically the same size. She did notice that each room had been decorated with a specific theme in mind.

This is like a fancy hotel.

Ana tried to imagine the place filled with guests at one of the Griffin's parties. She peered down the staircase. Andrew was sitting on the bottom step with his back toward her. His head was bent forward.

He must be looking at his cell phone.

110

"See anything interesting?" her voice echoed. Andrew's head popped up instantly. He twisted around to see her. He wasn't smiling. "I'm through with the second floor and am heading up to the third level. If you want to wait up here, there are some large comfortable looking chairs. Just wanted you to know." He turned around and went back to checking emails.

"Thank you, but I'm fine right here. Have fun exploring your mansion," he called without looking at her.

Ana licked her lips and glanced around. At the end of the wide hall to her left she saw a staircase leading upward.

That's how you get up to the third floor.

Even though this staircase was much narrower than the grand one, it was still gorgeous. It, too, had a carved, dark wooden banister. Ana looked at the steps that were covered with dust. And tracks.

"Here we go," she whispered. The thick carpet on the wooden stairs muffled the creaks and groans as she made her way upward. Upon reaching the top, she discovered more antique furniture attractively arranged. The walls were covered with framed, professional-looking group and individual photos of the Griffins. As Ana walked along, she studied each one and noticed that the family aged from photo to photo. She thought about the Griffins.

This was where your private bedrooms were.

On the opposite wall was an array of personal vacation pictures.

"These must have been some of their favorites," she said. Some of the photos had captions underneath. Ana narrated some of them. "Skiing in the Alps. Riding camels in front of the pyramids. Splashing in the waves on some exotic beach. Visiting the lost city of *Machu Picchu* in Peru. Standing in front of the...oh, yeah, the Eifel Tower, and..." Ana moved to another group of photos. She recognized them immediately. "Oh, cool! These are on the Galapagos Islands. There's Beatrice with the iguana." Ana saw a photo of the family surrounded by several huge tortoises. She leaned in closer to study the ancient creatures. "I wonder which one of them is Ricky?" Other memories of the family she had gleaned from studying the newspapers flooded back into her mind.

I almost forgot how much I love all of you. This was your home. How many times did you stand here and look at these?

Ana made her way to the widest part of the balcony. Carefully, she inched over to the rail and looked down into the cavernous entrance hall.

Oh, wow!

Scanning the whole floor, she noticed at the far end there was an enormous dark wood cabinet, instead of a conversation area, and there were only five doors, instead of nine—two on the right, two on the left and one directly behind her. Like on the second floor, the wrap-around balcony gave access to each room.

If there are only five rooms up here, they must all be huge.

Ana saw that the door on the far-right side had been left open. She made her way over to it and peeked inside.

This must have been Mrs. Griffin's personal parlor and office. Looks like Mr. Hill checked it over, too.

Ana entered and picked up an overturned dainty-looking chair with pink, patterned upholstery. She moved it back beside a small, delicate table. Paintings with gorgeous frames that had been removed from the walls lay scattered around. She picked up each one and tried to put it back on the wall where she supposed it had once been. Beautiful, dusty, white lace drapes graced the windows. An antique-looking desk and chair stood in a corner of the room in front of expertly crafted pearl-white, built in shelves. Ana walked over and closed the doors to the cabinets. On top of the desk was a typewriter, which Ana had only seen in movies. Touching the 'A" key, she pressed it downwards and watched as the thin, metal arm arched upwards. She removed her finger and the metal arm fell back into place.

That is so cool!

Glancing up from the typewriter, she saw a closed door on the far side of the room.

Well, hello!

Ana walked over to the door, grabbed the latch and tried several times to open it with no success. She looked for signs that Lawrence Hill had tried to pry it open, but there were none. After examining the rest of the room, Ana returned to the balcony walkway and proceeded to the next door. She reached out and tried the latch.

Locked. Oh, great. Now I'll have to find another key.

After examining the door closely, she could tell that there was nothing to indicate that Hill had tried to pry it open.

Well, I guess you had your limits, didn't you? You weren't ready to just break into this room, because that would have been illegal! Right, Mr. Attorney-at-law?

Ana looked back at the open door to Beatrice's parlor and then at the one in front of her. The truth dawned on her.

Wait a minute! This locked room has got to be... her bedroom.

Swallowing hard Ana backed away from it. Her vivid imagination that came from watching way too many movies kicked into high gear.

What if he left it exactly the way it was the day she died? What if he never went back in there? What if...

Her backward motion was halted by the rail of the balcony. Ana spun around and stared downwards into the gaping void of the enormous hall. "Uh!" she groaned and retreated a couple of steps. She rubbed her face with her hands and stood there staring at the door—actually relieved that it was locked.

*There's no way I'm going in **there** by myself.*

She considered asking Andrew, but then thought about her mother. "Mom! I'll ask Mom," she uttered under her breath, "she'll love it. Well, maybe not *love it*."

Turning to her right, Ana spied the one lone door on the long back wall.

That's got to be his room.

Chapter Ten

Ana inched her way back to the third-floor balcony rail and gazed downward. Andrew was still waiting patiently on the bottom step of the staircase. "Hey!" she called. He stood up and twirled around trying to see where she was. "Up here!" she laughed and waved.

"Oh! There you are! Are you almost finished?"

"No. I've still got a couple of rooms to go. It shouldn't take long." Ana couldn't see the expression on his face but could tell by his body language that he was getting tired of doing nothing. "Why don't you check out the bottom floor for bad guys?"

"Don't worry about me. Just let me know every now and then that you are still alive," he said and slumped back down on the step.

"Sounds like a plan," she called with a chuckle.

"Funny. Very funny," he grumbled.

Ana walked to the door that she supposed was Rudolph Griffin's bedroom.

What if it still looks like the day he died? I just hope it's not locked, too.

It wasn't. She slowly opened the door but wasn't prepared for what she saw.

"Goodness gracious!" The room was gigantic. Ana could instantly tell that it, too, had been thoroughly ransacked. Almost nothing was where it had originally been. "Why was I afraid that it might look like it did the day he died?" she whispered. "Lawrence Hill must have spent days in here." Things were scattered everywhere. Cabinet doors and drawers were left open. Every piece of furniture had been moved. Most of the chairs were lying on their sides. A couple of the huge paintings had been taken down and were leaning against the wall. Ana examined the walls and could tell by the difference in color on the dark wooden paneling where they had once hung.

To her far right was an enormous stone fireplace with an intricately carved mantel. Large, heavy-looking chairs and tables had once been arranged in front of it. The fabulous built-in shelves on either side of the fireplace had also been rifled. Ana tried to imagine Rudolph Griffin sitting in front of a roaring fire, but it was no use.

It was obvious that the massive four poster bed had been moved from the middle of the

118

room. She recalled the first time she had seen Hill in the mansion and had heard him moving something heavy upstairs. "I'll bet you almost broke your back with this bed," she joked, walked over and examined the detail of one of the posts. Looking around, she noticed a very thick Persian carpet that had also been carelessly folded up and shoved to the side. From the smears in the dust, Ana figured the bed had once been centered on the carpet.

"That's why you moved the bed," she shook her head in disgust. "Wow! How brilliant! What a perfect place for an 81-year-old man to hide his will!" she uttered sarcastically and added, "Duh!"

Ana gazed around the room. The vaulted, gothic ceiling was accented by brass chandeliers. Even though it was a chaotic mess, the furnishings in the room were lavish. To the left were two doors—one of which was open. Ana peeked inside and could tell that it was a very large walk-in closet with shelves and mirrors. The floor was littered with clothes, shoes, and other items. "What a nightmare!" she groaned and bent over to grab a shoe that was blocking the door. She almost tossed it out of the way but then hesitated. Examining it, she could tell that it was the left one of a pair and well-worn. She thought about Mr. Griffin. Looking around on the floor

119

she found the right one and picked it up. They were dark, heavy, leather dress shoes. They reminded her of the shoes that her father wore to work. Ana held them up to her nose and could smell the leather.

You wore these a lot. Were they one of your favorite pairs?

Ana placed them gently on the floor and, for some unknown reason, paired up all the other shoes, lining them up next to each other. After that, she began picking up clothes and hanging them back up where she supposed they might once have been. Other items she arranged on the dark wooden shelves to her left that reached from the floor to higher than her head. Ana made sure all the drawers and cabinet doors were shut.

Well, at least this closet is back in order.

Back in the bedroom, Anna stepped to the other door and opened it. It was the adjoining bathroom, which was more like an enormous, luxurious spa. "Mom will go nuts when she sees this," she laughed and added, "but I don't need to waste time in here. A bathroom is still just a bathroom."

Closing the door, she turned around and carefully scanned the enormous bedroom again—now from a different vantage point.

Ana didn't know why, but she felt like there was something she was supposed to see. To her left, a huge picture window filled most of the back wall. On her way over to it, out of the corner of her eye, one of the largest paintings in the room caught her attention. It was leaning against the wall. Ana walked over to it.

How cool is this? It's a castle.

She clicked on her flashlight and shined it on the painting to get a better look. "Oh, my!" she exclaimed. "It's not a painting at all. It's a photo. It's just been made to look like a painting. It's a real castle."

She walked over and stopped where she figured the bed once stood. Ana directed her gaze at the wall, where the large painting had been hanging before it was taken down.

This one was important to you. You could look at it without getting out of bed.

She scratched her chin and walked back over to the gigantic photo. "I wonder where it is?" Ana took a picture of it with her cell phone and checked the result. "That'll do just fine."

Gazing around the room once again, Ana saw the enormous rear window and moved toward it. "Oh, Wow! Wow! Wow!" she cried as the vista spread out in front of her. Finally, standing in the center of the window she looked down and gasped. All the visible landscaping had been designed and laid out with an undeniable central focal point. Everything was directed toward the gleaming white mausoleum.

Ana moved a chair closer to the window and sat down. Staring back and forth for maybe five minutes, she tried to take it all in. Her eyes settled back on the tomb. She recalled how beautiful it was inside. Finally, she shook her head.

Oh well, I need to get on with it.

She got up to go and headed for the door. Glancing around at everything one more time, Ana suddenly froze in her tracks.

Wait a minute.

A grouping of seven smaller framed family photos was arranged on the wall just to the left of the door. When she examined them, she almost exploded.

"It's the photo! The one they used for the family painting in Mr. Griffin's study. The one where he's looking at Ricky in the bushes!" The placement of the photo in the grouping seemed odd to her because it was to the left of the others.

"You're looking to the left! Are we doing this again? Do you want me to look in the direction you're looking?" The idea made perfect sense, so she turned and glanced down the wall.

It's another bunch of photos.

They were all of Beatrice—when she was young and beautiful. The central photo in the group showed her standing in front of the large window in her sitting room. Her right hand was extended head-high, holding onto the window casing. Ana covered her mouth to stifle a squeal, turned, and raced out of the room straight back to Beatrice's parlor.

She went immediately to the window and examined the casing. It was beautifully carved and reminded her of the window in Griffin's study.

"Where are you? Where are you?" she murmured as she leaned her head against the wall and moved her gaze up and down. "Where was her hand?" As soon as the question left her mouth, she saw it. It was the same color as the molding and blended in perfectly, but Ana Stilwell knew what she was looking for.

"Bingo!" she chuckled, reached up and snagged the end of a narrow metal object with her fingernail. Carefully she picked it out of its hiding place and dropped the key into her left hand. She quickly walked to the locked door, stuck the key in the lock and turned it.

Click!

Ana grabbed the doorknob but then stopped. She was shaking all over. Letting go, she backed away and plopped down on a very dusty chair.

"No. I need Mom to be with me when I go in there!" She stared at the door and noticed the key still sticking in the lock. Ana stood up, walked over and began to pull it out, but then hesitated.

Why do I need to take it with me or even hide it? The door is unlocked. I can get in. That's all that matters. Ol' Lawrence Hill isn't going to be up here snooping around anymore. I can just leave it in the lock until we get back.

Ana walked out onto the balcony walkway and looked at the two remaining doors on the opposite side. She decided not to bother Andrew.

He must be dying to leave by now.

Arriving at the first door, she tried turning the latch.

Well, hallelujah. It's open.

It appeared to be a very large family room. There were more framed photos of the Griffins' vacations and travel to famous places. Most had been taken down and were stacked on the floor. Just like almost every room in the mansion, this one was also a disaster. Books, some of them still open, had been simply dumped from the shelves. Other personal family mementos were strewn about. Dust was everywhere, as were Lawrence Hill's tracks and finger smudges. The scene made Ana angry. So angry that she began to cry.

You didn't care about the Griffins at all, did you? I'll bet after you helped him with his will, you couldn't wait for him to die.

She turned around. In front of her was a large, wide wooden cabinet. She walked over to it, pushed open the sliding doors and revealed a built-in television. Ana wiped her face with her sleeve and examined it. "It's an older one, but the screen is huge," she took a deep breath and managed a smile. "Connor will flip out when he sees this. I wonder if it still works?" Ana turned around and noticed a large chair that had obviously not been moved. It was the only one pointing directly toward the set. Her thoughts drifted back to Rudolph Griffin.

This must have been where you sat and watched TV—all by yourself.

She took a deep breath and wiped her face again.

You had all that money, but you didn't have anything you really cared about, once they were gone.

Ana slid the doors shut, walked over and looked out the window. The foreground was filled with the roof top of the first floor of the mansion complex. She allowed her gaze to continue across the huge, overgrown lawn toward the edge of the forest. Because there were not yet any leaves blocking her view, she could see faintly through the trees in the distance.

"What is that?" There was a long, dark structure that caught her attention. Ana cupped her hands on the window to block out the glare.

"Oh, my goodness! It's the wall! The wall at the creek!" She quickly covered her mouth. Ana drew her eyes back toward the mansion across the lawn in an imaginary line.

That's where the tunnel is! That's why he built it where he did. It's the shortest distance from the mansion to the wall. I need to check it out. Why didn't I think of this sooner?

Ana walked out of the family room and opened the door to the next room.

"Oh, my, NO!!" she covered her scream. It was Lewis' bedroom. A huge, life-size, framed photo of him in his captain's uniform lay leaning on its side against the wall. On the opposite wall was a large, framed print of him riding on Ricky on the grounds of the estate. "There it is! The other photo!" She remembered finding the two, almost identical photos of him on the tortoise in the town's old newspapers.

Through tear-filled eyes, Ana surveyed the scene in front of her. Very personal items—

trophies, framed memories, and photos from Lewis' life—were scattered everywhere. Only a few were still hanging on the walls. Most had been carelessly tossed here and there. On the floor to the right of his bed was a large, thickly framed something lying face down. Ana picked it up, turned it over and screamed. It was the wooden shadow box containing the tri-folded flag that had been draped on Lewis' coffin.

"Oh, dear God! Help me!" Ana couldn't hold it in any longer. She stood there shaking, sobbing, and furious—at Lawrence Hill. In the distance she heard Andrew calling her name. Seconds later, she could make out his heavy footsteps as he bounded up the stairs and raced down the hall.

"Ana? Ana? Where are you? Are you okay?" he cried and ran into the room. She spun around and raised her hand up in the air. Her face was still soaking wet with tears.

"I'm okay! I'm okay!" she said, still shaking. "I didn't mean to scream. I'm sorry I scared you." She was clutching the box-framed flag to her chest. "I knew one of these rooms had to be Lewis' bedroom, but I wasn't prepared to find it..." She waved her hand around the room and showed him the flag, "like this! Not like this." Ana shook her head and slumped down on the floor. "I don't know what I was thinking."

Andrew walked over and knelt beside her. Finally, she shook her head and took a deep breath.

"Are you okay?" he asked softly.

"I'm fine. I'll be all right," she said bluntly.

"Do you want me to stay up here with you?"

"No," she said without looking at him. "We need to go. I've seen more than enough for one day."

"I agree," said Andrew.

"What time is it?" she blinked away the remaining tears and wiped her face with her hands.

Andrew checked his watch. "It's only 4:43." She motioned to him and he helped her stand up. Ana gently laid the shadow box with the flag on Lewis's bed and headed toward the door. Neither of them said anything as they made their way down and out of the mansion. Ana was still very upset. She was also careful to not make eye-contact with her bodyguard as they got into her Mercedes.

Turning out of the estate driveway onto Griffin Avenue, Andrew glanced over at her. "Are you all right?"

Ana sighed but didn't look at him. "Sure. I'm fine."

"Would you like to go get some ice cream or something?" he offered.

Ana turned, quickly glanced at him and immediately went back to staring out the window. "Do I look that bad? What's wrong? Are you worried what Mom might say if she sees me like this?"

"Oh, I just thought some Chocolate Mint might cheer you up," he stared straight ahead. At the next intersection, he didn't turn toward home. Ana sat up. After a couple of miles, he made another turn to the right and then back to the left.

"Ice Cream Palace?"

"Where else?" he smiled. "You want one scoop or two?"

"We better make it two," she mumbled. After receiving their order at the drive-thru window, they drove along without saying a word. Finally, between licks, Andrew broke the silence.

"Look. I know seeing Lewis' bedroom really upset you, but there's something else going on here. I've never seen you like this. What is it, Ana? What's wrong? I've got to know."

Ana didn't respond. She stared out her window and slowly ate her Chocolate Mint. He pulled over to the side of the road and finished his cone. She could feel him trying to read her brain through the back of her head. Ana closed her eyes.

"I'm not leaving this spot until you tell me what's going on."

"If you must know, I'm furious," she finally confessed. "And I was praying, asking Jesus to help me forgive him."

"Him?" exclaimed Andrew. "Forgive him?" Ana didn't respond. After several moments of silence, he reached over and took her by the shoulder, turning her to face him. "You know who was in the mansion, don't you?"

Ana held up her ice cream cone and slowly took a lick of it. She fixed her gaze on Andrew and narrowed her eyes.

"Oh, yes."

By the stunned expression on his face, she could tell that he was dying to know the identity of the intruder, but she also knew that he knew that she was not one to reveal information before she was ready.

"Won't you...?" he began but didn't finish his question.

Ana shook her head. "I'm not ready to tell you who he is. Not yet, anyway." She noticed the scowl on his face. "But I can tell you that he does not know that I know who he is. And since I found the will and he didn't, I can't think that he would ever risk coming back to the mansion."

"But he left his fingerprints everywhere," countered Andrew. "That's got to be his biggest worry. We need to get them documented. That way we can prove it was him!"

"I can't imagine that he's ever committed a real crime or even been arrested," she added. "So, he's probably never been fingerprinted by the police, right?"

Andrew groaned, started the car, reached up, and adjusted the rear-view mirror to check for oncoming traffic. "You watch too many movies, you know that?" he mumbled and pulled out into the street.

"I can't help it," Ana took another lick of her ice cream cone. "Dad makes us watch old detective movies."

Chapter Eleven

In school the next day, the bell rang, signaling the end of third period. Carter Hudson was in the hall waiting on her when she exited the classroom. His head shot up when he saw her. She walked toward him and gave her head a pleasant, but slightly curious wiggle.

"Hey. What's up?"

Carter leaned in close and put his head right next to hers. He smelled like DOVE soap, and to be perfectly honest, Ana had never liked the smell of DOVE soap...until now.

"Are you in some kind of trouble?" he whispered.

"What?" Ana stepped back and stared at him. "What are you talking about?"

"Well," he looked around to make sure no one could hear them. "I was walking down the hall yesterday after school, and I caught a glimpse of you and Ms. Quillian in her classroom. The door was closed, so I couldn't hear what she was saying, but you were sitting in a desk, and she was walking back and forth, waving her hand at some map. I know it's none of my business, but are you okay?"

Ana shook her head. "Yes. I'm fine."

"Well, that's good to hear." Carter rolled his eyes and then just stood there staring at her—waiting. Ana studied his face and could tell he was burning up with curiosity.

Why can't I tell him what I've been doing? I don't care if he knows everything. I need to start trusting somebody with all of this.

She leaned in closer to him. "There was a small label with some German words on the bottom of a crystal vase I found at the estate. Ms. Quillian told me what they meant and showed me on the map of Germany where the vase was probably made."

"Are you serious?" he stammered.

Ana grinned and nodded. "Uh, huh. And that's not all," she whispered, "I found it inside the mausoleum behind the mansion. It was on top of Beatrice Griffin's tomb." She bit her bottom lip and Carter's mouth fell open. Ana could tell he was trying desperately to process what she had just revealed to him. Finally, he swallowed hard and shook his head.

"You are absolutely the...," he paused. Ana could tell he was searching frantically for the appropriate adjective. She closed her eyes and waited for him to finish. After three, long seconds of silence, she peeked and saw his radiant face. "...coolest person I know!" The bell rang again, and he turned to head to class.

"Carter?" she called. He spun around and she walked up to him. "I found something else that I need to show Ms. Quillian. If you want to, you can meet me in her classroom after school."

"Oh, wow! Don't worry. I'll be there!" he blurted out and took off running.

* * * * *

After school, Ana peered through the glass window in the classroom door to make sure that Ms. Quillian was still in her room. Her history teacher was seated at her desk at the front.

Good. There she is. It looks like she's working on something.

Ana was waiting for Carter to arrive so that they could enter the room together. Turning around, she saw him racing down the hall toward her. About ten feet away from her, he slowed down and threw both of his arms up into the air. She could tell he was upset.

"Old man Lindsay made us pick up every scrap of paper and junk off the floor before we could leave! Can you believe that?" he growled.

"How come?" she asked.

"Oh, he said he was tired of teaching in a pig sty." Ana snickered. Carter was still trying to catch his breath and stared at her. "What's a pig sty?"

"I think it's a nasty place where pigs live," she laughed. "That's what my mother calls my brother's room. And it is always a total mess!"

He laughed and peeked through the door. "Is Ms. Quillian still here?"

"Yes. I was waiting for you to get here, before I went in. Are you calmed down enough yet?" she teased.

"Yes, Miss Stilwell. I'm fine."

He opened the door and let Ana go in first. Ms. Quillian glanced up from the papers she was grading and removed her glasses. "Well, hello again!" she nodded in Carter's direction. "I see this time you've brought Mr. Hudson with you." Ana noticed an inquisitive gleam in her history teacher's eyes. "Have you found something else?"

"Yes, ma'am." Ana had already brought up the photo of the castle on her phone and held it out for her teacher to see. "At first, I thought it was a painting, but it's not. It's a photo of a real place."

"Hmm. Very interesting. May I enlarge the photo?"

"Oh, sure," said Ana, but then quickly corrected herself, "uh, yes ma'am."

Ms. Quillian grinned and zoomed in on the castle. Without looking up, she stated, "Well, it's definitely European." She zoomed the photo back out. "Let's see if there's anything in the surrounding landscape that I recognize." Ana glanced over at Carter and made a goofy-looking, wide-grin smiley face that meant she was excited. He made the same face back at her. They almost broke out laughing, but then controlled themselves. They made stern-looking faces at one another and turned their attention back to their history teacher. Finally, Ms. Quillian put her glasses back on and handed the cell phone to Ana.

"It's not a large castle, but it is very old and intact. It's also probably privately owned. It could be in Germany, Austria, extreme northern Italy, or possibly even Switzerland." She stood up and went to the blackboard. Reaching up she pulled down the map of

Western Europe. She pointed to the countries in question.

"Well, that's a good start," said Ana, trying to sound positive.

"Yes, it is," replied her teacher. "And it's also situated on a small, forested hill overlooking a major river, so that narrows it down a bit further." Then she added, "but a lot of castles were built near rivers. That way they could charge money to barges and ships wanting to pass."

"What happened if they didn't pay?" asked Carter.

Ms. Quillian opened her eyes wide and glared at the two of them—waiting for the lighted fuse to reach the powder. "Boom!" she thundered. Ana and Carter jumped straight up, shocked by the concussion of the blast. The teacher shook her head. "They would blow them out of the water with their cannons!"

At first, Ana was stunned, but then laughed. "Oh, wow!"

"That is so cool!" Carter muttered under his breath.

Ms. Quillian rubbed her chin and indicated the course of a long river on the map with her finger. "I'm almost positive your castle is not on the Rhine, because I saw all of them when I was there," she explained. "Would you mind texting me that photo? That way I can work on it and see what I can come up with."

"Oh, thank you!" cried Ana. Ms. Quillian gave her the cell number and after a couple of taps on her phone, the photo was sent and received. Ana and Carter thanked Ms. Quillian again and walked out into the hall.

"I've never seen her get this excited about anything," he remarked as they strolled toward the front door. Ana giggled.

"She's a lot of fun once you get to know her." They exited the school and started down the steps. Ana saw Andrew and Connor waiting in the Mercedes. "How are you getting home?"

"Same as always," muttered Carter. "On my own two feet."

"Would you like to ride with us?" she offered.

"Are you kidding?" he stopped and laughed. "Ride with you in your chauffeur-driven Mercedes? You bet! Just let me ask my mom." He yanked out his phone and called his mother.

"He's not my chauffeur," corrected Ana. "He's my bodyguard." She left Carter standing on the sidewalk and walked toward the car.

Andrew opened the door and got out. "Is anything wrong?" he asked.

"No," she pointed back at her classmate. "I asked Carter if he wanted us to drop him off at his house. He's asking his mom. It's not that far out of our way," she smiled and then added, "that is, if you don't mind."

Andrew snapped to attention and saluted. "Your wish is my command, Miss Stilwell."

Ana glared at him and mouthed, *Stop it!*

He silently mouthed back, *Yes, ma'am!*

"Mom says it's okay," Carter beamed and hurried over to them.

"Why don't we sit in the back seat," suggested Ana. "Connor. You get to ride up front."

"Hot dog! Shotgun!" he shrieked and lunged over the seat. Ana frowned, but then out of the corner of her eye caught Carter's questioning glance at Andrew. She followed his stare and saw Andrew wink back at him. She didn't let on that she understood their signals.

Carter opened the rear door. "After you, Miss Stilwell."

"Oh, thank you, Mr. Hudson." Ana moved gracefully like a princess taking her seat in a carriage. Carter carefully closed the door,

140

strutted around, and got in on the other side. Through the window she saw a group of girls passing by the car. The looks on their faces, with their mouths gaping wide open, was priceless. As the engine roared to life, she glanced over at Carter. She could tell he hadn't noticed the girls. He was too busy feeling the leather seats and checking out the interior of the luxurious vehicle.

"Man!" he purred. "Now, THIS is the way to ride home from school!"

Ana looked out her window and sighed. *Boys.*

Chapter Twelve

After dropping Carter off at his house, Ana stayed in the back seat and allowed her younger brother to continue riding in the front.

"Andrew, I need to go by the estate on our way home please," she informed him. "I want to check on something outside. It shouldn't take more than fifteen or twenty minutes."

"No problem," he said without turning around.

"Can I go, too?" begged Connor.

"Of course," replied Ana, "but you must promise that you will stay close to the car and do exactly whatever Andrew tells you to do."

"Yippee!" he hollered. "I promise!"

"And I don't want you following me," she added.

"Okay, I won't." He was still bouncing around in his seat.

"And under no circumstances are you to bother Ricky, if you see him," she stated.

"What's circumstances mean?" he asked.

"Just leave Ricky alone!" commanded Ana and made *the face* at him.

"Yes, ma'am," he turned and gazed out the window.

"Is he allowed to breathe?" teased Andrew. "I just need to know, since I'm going to have to watch him."

Ana almost responded but didn't. In the distance she recognized the long stone wall of the Griffin Estate.

* * * * *

Andrew parked the Mercedes beside the mansion. Connor jumped out and started running around. "Wow!" he exclaimed, waving his hands back and forth. "Just look at this place. It's all cleaned up!"

Ana got out and motioned to Andrew to come closer, so her brother wouldn't hear. "Please keep him on this side of the mansion. I want to check out the orchard and see what the other side looks like."

"That shouldn't be a problem. I'll suggest we walk down to see the tennis courts and the swimming pool. How long do you think you'll be?'

"That's a great idea. I'll need maybe twenty minutes, if that long," she smiled and pulled out her whistle. "I'll give a couple of toots on this, if I need you."

They winked at each other and said in unison, "Sounds like a plan."

"Hey Connor!" Andrew called. "Let's go see what the swimming pool looks like!"

Ana saw her brother take off running across the huge lawn in the direction of the pool house. "Don't let him jump in!" she yelled.

"I won't," hollered Andrew as he took off jogging after Connor.

Ana made her way around to the far side of the mansion— the side that had not been touched by the lawn service yet. The weeds and grass were still

high, and the dark trees of the forgotten orchard loomed over her head. Broken, fallen limbs were strewn here and there. Ignored shrubs and huge ornamental plants fought to take over everything. Finally, she made it to where she could see the windows of the third floor—the family entertainment room and Lewis' bedroom—over the roof top of the lower level. Ana lowered her gaze to the first-floor level and the windowless outside wall in front of her.

That must be where those storage rooms are.

With her back to the building, Ana began walking in a straight line away from the mansion. At the edge of the woods, she slowed down and began carefully picking her way through the trees, fallen limbs and undergrowth. Pausing to get her bearings, Ana glanced up.

"There it is!" she squealed. About twenty yards in front of her was the stone wall. To her left through the trees she could see the corner. From where she was standing, she could tell that the corner wasn't the end of the property at all, but simply skirted around the bluff above the creek and then continued in the same direction. Ana quickened her pace and soon was standing at the base of it. The top cap of the wall was several feet above her outstretched grasp. "There is no way I could ever climb over this without a ladder or something," she remarked. Remaining perfectly quiet, she finally heard the faint babbling sounds of the creek.

"Wow. The boulder and the door to the tunnel are just on the other side." Ana reached out and rubbed the weathered surface of the stones. Turning around, she could make out the mansion through the trees. "It's hard to believe that now it all belongs to me." Ana shook her head to clear it.

Okay. That's enough strolling down memory lane. I've got to figure out where the large room in the tunnel is.

She pointed her arm in the direction she needed to begin walking and measuring.

It was 111 yards from the creek.

Though the going was not easy, Ana started taking giant steps away from the wall. Suddenly she stopped.

Oh, wait! The tunnel didn't go straight. It curved slightly to the left. I won't ever forget that! So, I need to try to make a gradual swerve to the right and then back.

She returned to the wall and stood with her back against it.

"One, two, three, four..." Ana counted each stride out loud, careful to make a long arching curve. She was glad when she finally exited the woods and was walking across the overgrown lawn. Without pausing, she kept walking and counting and getting closer and closer to the mansion. When she got to where she figured the large room was, she stopped and gazed down at the ground.

It's got to be right here under my feet.

Ana glanced to her left toward the orchard. She decided that she should have a fence put up around the whole area to keep people out. Rubbing her chin, she grinned.

And to keep Ricky from just wandering off.

Looking back directly in front of her, she noticed the windowless lower level wall of the mansion again. It wasn't more than thirty feet away from her. Moving her eyes slowly upward, she tried to picture where the wooden door and the stairs up to the secret passageway had to be. Turning her body toward the right, Ana again studied the ground, wishing she had x-ray vision.

I can't believe it! I was in that tunnel, and I even let out string to measure the distance! But I didn't think I would need it. Brilliant, Ana. Absolutely brilliant.

Trying desperately to remember how far it was, she walked over to where she guessed the entrance to the tunnel had to be.

It was probably thirty feet to the wall with the markings where I found Ricky's name.

Ana paced off the distance and stopped again.

Let's see. After Ricky's wall, I walked just a little way, and then the tunnel curved sharply to the left.

Looking at the ground, Ana took several more steps, adjusted her body to the correct bearings. She held up her arm like a pointer. The rear corner of the mansion appeared to be about forty or fifty feet directly in front of her.

"That's where the metal plate door is! It's directly below that corner of the mansion!" she squealed. Ana sprinted to the edge of the building and halted. Examining the base of the corner of the mansion, she hunted for anything that seemed out of the ordinary.

That door has got to be down there, right about here. But the question is: Where does the tunnel go on the other side?

Raising her head, Ana peered down the back wall of the mansion looking for clues— anything. She saw the huge rear terrace. Ana continued to let her gaze swing to the right. In

148

the distance was the white marble mausoleum. Ana remembered seeing it from the enormous window in Rudolph Griffin's bedroom.

It's in the center of everything.

CHapter THirteeN

When Ana and Andrew walked into
Lewistowne Elementary School the next
morning, almost every girl they passed in the
crowded hall turned and smiled at Ana.

What is going on?

She thought about going back outside to check
the name on the front of the building, just to
make sure she was in the right place.

"You did bring me to the right school, didn't
you?" She quipped to her bodyguard.

"Why?" he asked. Before she could answer,
another girl—Rebecca Hightower—a member of
Skylar's gang, waved at her.

"Hey, Ana!" Other girls chimed in like they had
been trained by a professional greeting service.

"Oh, hey!" she replied, nodding her head to
acknowledge each one. At her locker, she
quickly spun the dial back and forth, opened
the door, and crammed her jacket inside.
Removing the books and items she needed for
math class, Ana closed the door and stared

straight into the face of a radiant Skylar Perkins.

"Good morning, Ana!" she beamed.

"Hey," stuttered Ana in response.

Skylar moved to within inches of Ana's face. "Thank you so much! My dad told us this morning at breakfast that he got the job at the newspaper, and he loves it. He's even making more money than he was in his old job." Reaching out, she grabbed Ana with both arms in a bear hug. "And it's all because of you! I am so, so sorry for the way I treated you. You are the best! The best!"

The other girls in Skylar's gang quickly gathered in a circle around the two of them, cooing and nodding. Ana managed an odd grin, as Skylar shook her back and forth.

This is really embarrassing.

Suddenly the bell rang. Skylar released Ana and patted her on the back. "See you around!" She turned and headed down the hall. Each member of her gang tapped Ana on the shoulder in the exact same spot.

Ana noticed Andrew several feet away—grinning. She knew he had seen the whole thing and walked up to him. He shook his body, bugged-out his eyes, and stuck out his tongue like he was being squeezed to death. Ana punched him in the arm.

"Stop it!" she demanded.

"I don't know what to say," he snickered. "Wow. I've never witnessed an honest-to-goodness female appreciation ritual before. It was quite moving," he paused for a couple seconds and then added, "and that it was that horrible, mean girl who you can't stand... wow! Talk about a miracle!"

"She's just happy that her dad got a job," Ana huffed and began walking toward her classroom. Andrew followed close behind.

"Did **you** call the newspaper and set it up?" he prodded.

"No, I did not!" Ana didn't slow down or turn to look at him.

"It wasn't you?" he teased.

"No." Ana halted abruptly, and Andrew almost ran into her. She glared at him "It wasn't me!" The glare turned into a snicker. "I asked Chuck, and he called the newspaper."

"That's splitting hairs," Andrew joked.

"No," she held her finger up in the air in front of his face. "That's being accurate."

After school, Ana quickly finished her homework and headed downstairs to find her mother. Instead of yelling for her like Connor would, she first checked the kitchen and then the living room.

There you are.

One of her mom's favorite TV programs, about some couple searching for a house somewhere, was on. Instead of interrupting, Ana walked over and sat down beside her on the couch.

"I'll bet they choose house number three," Nancy Stilwell said pointing at the screen. "It's smaller than she really wants, but her husband keeps saying that it's within their budget and that they can add space." Ana didn't respond, but instead just enjoyed watching her mother.

You love programs like this, dreaming about living in some other place, in some other house, and wondering about what that would be like. Well Mom, you are going to absolutely love what I'm about to ask you to do.

The couple in the program made their decision and her mother threw up her hands.

"I told you they would choose number three!" she exclaimed and turned toward Ana. "It's always about the money." Ana watched the expression on her mother's face go through a series of contortions, before she burst out laughing. "Ha! How silly of me?"

Ana stared at her. "What do you mean, Mom?"

"Here I am watching some show about some people I don't even know, or care about, trying to choose which house they can afford, and here you sit—my daughter— with enough money to buy any house in any place in any country on earth—my daughter, who owns a gigantic, gorgeous mansion."

Ana grinned at her but didn't say a word. She wanted to let her calm down a little.

Her mother stood up, turned off the TV and looked at Ana. "Do you need me to do something, sweetheart?"

"Yes, ma'am." The grin vanished from her face. "Would you, please, go with me and Andrew to the mansion this afternoon? I want to begin cleaning it up and would love to get your ideas. I need you to go through it with me and tell me what you think."

Nancy Stilwell sat back down on the sofa and stared at her daughter.

"Are you serious?"

"Yes, ma'am. But I don't need Connor to go with us, if you know what I mean." She shook her head. "I don't want to have to deal with him."

"Oh, I agree. I'll call Johnny Ralston's mother and see if your brother can spend the whole afternoon over there."

"That's a great idea," agreed Ana. "That way Connor will be happy and won't care about where we are going." Then she added, "Of course, Andrew will need to drive us. I'll let him know, as soon as you know something."

Nancy reached out and hugged her daughter. "Thank you for asking me to go. It means a lot to me. Your father and I are very proud of you and all the decisions you've made. We just want to help in any way we can."

"I know," she buried her face into her mother's shoulder. "I love you so much." Then she pulled back and laughed. "This'll be like one of your house-shows on TV!"

Nancy Stilwell shook her head. "I don't believe I have ever seen a show about a girl your age and her mother making plans to clean up a huge mansion."

Ana chuckled. "Well, maybe we should get someone to film the whole thing. Maybe WE can be on TV."

Her mother raised her right shoulder and patted her hair. "Well now, that would call for a trip to the *Girls and Curls Beauty Salon*, don't you think?" She picked up her cell phone and tapped in the Ralston's number. As she waited for someone to answer, Ana's mother began flipping her hair with her hand. Ana recognized the sign.

She's happy. I am so glad I asked her to go to the mansion.

"Hello Jennifer?" Nancy Stilwell enjoyed talking with Connor's best friend's mother. Before long she was chatting and waving her hand in the air.

Uninterested in the conversation, Ana casually stared out the window. Suddenly, she remembered the real reason why she had asked her mother to go with her—she didn't want to be alone when she entered the bedroom of Rudolph Griffin's dead wife. Ana pursed her lips, scratched the side of her head, and stared at her mother.

Should I tell her now?

Nancy Stilwell glanced over at Ana, nodded and gave her a *thumbs up*. Ana stuck her thumb up in the air, managed a weak smile, and nodded back.

I'll just wait... I sure hope she doesn't wig out on me.

* * * * *

Even though her mother had been over to the estate a couple of times before, she had not seen it since the lawn service crew had made such improvements.

"Oh, Ana!" Nancy cried as they drove through the service entrance. "Just look! It's gorgeous!"

Ana glanced over at Andrew. He smiled and kept his eyes on the long curving road.

"Well, Mr. Johnson did say that everything had been neglected for so long, that it could take a while for them to get it all back in shape," Ana explained, gazing out the window to her right. "We just need to be patient."

"I am so glad you invited me to come." The remark made Ana turn around. Her mother's face was glowing.

"Me too, Mom."

* * * * *

"Has the inside changed since your birthday party?" her mother asked at they strolled up the front steps.

"I'm afraid not," replied Ana, shaking her head. They watched as Andrew unlocked the front door and followed him inside.

"Well, that's why I'm here, so that we can figure out what needs to be done."

Ana grinned at the tone of her mother's remark.

She's in full mother-knows-best mode.

"Well, that's why I wanted you to come," Ana stated seriously. "I mean, just look at this place!" She stepped forward and waved her hands back and forth in front of her.

"Oh, my!" Nancy Stilwell exclaimed and strolled out into the center of the cavernous room. "I had forgotten how big and fabulous it is!" She moved over to one of the expensive pieces of furniture and wiped her finger through the dust. "I thought we did a better job of cleaning it up for your birthday."

"No, Mrs. Stilwell," said Andrew. "Don't you remember? Ana said she wanted to try and leave everything just the way it was."

"Oh, yes. That's right!" she glanced at her daughter, "but you never told me why." Ana walked over to where she was standing and pointed to the print made by a hand much larger than her mother's.

"Fingerprints." she explained. "Chuck said we need to have a detective come in here and make a record of them. They're all over the house," she paused to gaze up at the third floor where Lewis Griffin's room was, "...on everything."

* * * * *

When she and her mother were in the mansion before, they had focused on getting the grand dining hall ready for Ana's twelfth birthday and had simply ignored everything else. Now, one-by-one, they examined each of the rooms that opened into the main hall.

When they entered the music room with the grand piano, her mother stopped in the door. "Wow! I'm sure this place used to be stunning! But now, every room is a complete wreck!"

"I know," said Ana, throwing up her hands. "What do you think I ought to do?"

"Well, you will probably want to hire a professional cleaning and restoration service, or services, that specialize in this sort of thing," she gestured downward with her hand and then waved it around. "The floors, the carpets, this gorgeous furniture, the drapes, the piano..." The list grew as she spun around, describing the scene in front of them. "The fixtures, the antiques, the books, the shelves, all the beautiful photos and exotic, priceless doo dads and..." she pointed to one of the enormous, lavishly framed paintings, "and all of these horribly expensive looking paintings!"

Ana shook her head. "It is something, isn't it?"

"Oh, yes," her mother sighed. "It definitely is something."

Andrew led the way as they inspected the rest of the lower level: staff quarters, the huge kitchen with adjoining pantries, the grand dining hall, and another much smaller personal dining room.

"I think this is probably where the Griffins ate most of their meals." Ana opened one of the cabinets filled with less lavish plates, bowls, cups, and glasses. Her mother nodded in agreement.

After passing by several guest rooms, they finally reached the rear hallway. Ana walked past the secret passageway entrance to one of the storage rooms she had discovered. Pushing open the door, she went to the cabinet filled with towels. Nancy entered the room, but Andrew stayed in the hall.

"Mom, wait until you see what's in here!"

"Oh wow!" exclaimed her mother. She reached in, pulled out one of the very thick towels and

160

examined it. "They are excellent quality and probably cost a lot of money," she looked at Ana. "But they may have deteriorated over time and could just fall apart when washed."

"Really?" frowned Ana.

"I'm afraid so," her mother replaced the towel and walked to another cabinet. It was filled with washcloths and smaller towels. "These are very high quality, too," she said as she rubbed her hand over the top of them. Ana saw her turn around and smile. "But we won't know for sure, until we send them through the washing machine. You want to try some and see what happens?"

"Oh, yes!" beamed Ana. "I would love to know if they're any good."

Ana watched as her mother removed a couple of towels, washcloths, and other items. "This ought to be enough," she smiled.

As they exited the room, Ana took the stack from her mother and handed it to Andrew. "Would you please hold on to these for us while we look around upstairs?" she batted her eyes at him and grinned.

"Hmm," he grimaced and stared at her. "Yes, ma'am. No problem."

They walked back to the main room with Andrew marching right behind them. Twice, Ana glanced back over her shoulder at him. Each time she did, he stuck his nose up in the air, frowned, and held the stack out in front of him.

I wish I could make a video of him. He has no idea how funny he looks. Mr. Collins, the butler.

The three of them arrived back in the huge entrance hall near the bottom of the main staircase.

"What is that room over there?" asked Ana's mother, pointing at the closed door of the only room left to be inspected on the ground floor.

Ana replied without any emotion. "That's Mr. Griffin's study. It's fabulous, too, and it's a complete mess."

"Just like every other room in the house," her mother noted.

"Of course!" Ana acknowledged and started toward the door. "Would you like to see it?"

"No, not right now." Her mother gazed up the steps of the magnificent stairway. "I'd rather see what's upstairs." Ana glanced at Andrew and made a face he had seen many times before.

"I know." He plopped down on the bottom step, placed the stack of towels and other linens beside him, and pulled out his cell phone without looking up. "Let me know if I can help."

"I've got my whistle and my mother, what more could I need?" teased Ana.

Andrew said something under his breath, leaned back on the steps, and ignored her.

"Come on, Mom. Let's strut up the staircase like royalty."

"Oh, Ana!" her mother cried, but followed her daughter's lead.

Halfway up the stairs, Ana turned and peeked back at Andrew. He was watching them and shaking his head.

CHapter FourteeN

Since all the rooms on the second floor were basically the same, it didn't take long for Ana and her mother to complete the inspection. Back on the main landing, Nancy glanced around and saw the staircase to her left. "That one must lead up to the next floor." She pointed and began walking toward it.

Ana followed her without responding. Nancy started climbing the stairs. At the top, her mother turned and grinned at her. "This place was like a fancy hotel."

"That's exactly what I thought the first time I saw it," Ana blurted out, but it was too late. Her mother stared at her. "So, you've already been up here?" Ana cut her eyes away from her mother and nodded. Seconds ticked away. "You've already seen everything, haven't you?"

"Yes, ma'am," she finally confessed but was unable to conceal her nervousness. "That is...almost everything." Her mother pulled back from her. Ana knew that she had read the expression on her face. "Oh, Mom!" she buried her head into her mother. Nancy

Stilwell put her arms around her and hugged her tightly.

"What is it, Ana?" she asked softly. "What's the matter?"

After a few seconds, Ana muttered quietly. "It's their bedrooms...it's where they lived. The last time I was up here, I broke down when I went into Lewis' room. It brought back so many memories."

Nancy patted her daughter's back. "Well, that's to be expected." Then she gently pushed Ana away from her and cupped her face in her hands, just like she always did when Ana was upset. "You care very deeply about him and his memory, don't you?"

"Yes, ma'am," she lowered her eyes. "But that's not what's bothering me this time."

"What do you mean?" asked her mother.

Ana struggled to get her emotions back under control. "I've already searched all the rooms up here except one."

"Why didn't you search it?"

Ana squinted at her. "Because it's got to be the bedroom of Rudolph Griffin's dead wife, Beatrice," her voice grew in intensity. "I didn't want to go in there by myself, because of what I might find."

Nancy Stilwell reached out and hugged her daughter close to her. They both stood there at the top of the stairs for at least a minute. Finally, her mother took a deep breath. "Okay, then. Let's go see what's in Beatrice Griffin's bedroom."

When they got to the widest area of the balcony, she stopped and pointed to the door behind them. "That one leads to Mr. Griffin's bedroom suite," she explained and gestured at the first door to their left. "That room was the family entertainment room and that last one over there was Lewis' bedroom." Ana pointed at the doors to the right. "Mrs. Griffin's rooms are over there."

Ana led the way around the balcony walkway past the closed door to the second door, which was still open. "This was her office and sitting room."

"Oh, my!" her mother exclaimed as she entered the room. "How beautiful is this?" She and Ana took a moment to inspect everything.

"See?" Ana walked over and pointed at an exquisite desk and chair. "I think this was her office—where she wrote letters and stuff."

166

"You're probably right," agreed her mother and turned around. She pointed with her right hand. "Is that the door to her bedroom?"

"I think so," said Ana. "But I don't know for sure, because, like I said I haven't been in there yet."

"Well, let's not put it off any longer," proposed her mother. "Come on. Let's do it!" She marched over to the door. "Do you want me to open it, or do you want to?"

Ana shook her head. "Mom, I have opened so many doors in this place, that it's okay with me if you do the honors this time."

Nancy bit her lower lip, put her hand on the latch, pressed it downward, and very slowly opened the door. The room inside was completely dark, because the window shades had been lowered all the way to the floor and the drapes were closed shut.

"Just a minute," Ana said, pulled her flashlight out of her pocket, clicked it on, and shined it around the wall. "There's a window over there," she announced.

"Your flashlight!" cried her mother. "The one you bought with your birthday money!" She covered her mouth with her hand. "This is why you needed a flashlight! To explore the mansion. Your father and I thought you wanted it because your bedroom at home was too dark."

They walked over to the window. She held the flashlight while her mother pushed the drapes back and raised the shade. Light poured into Beatrice Griffin's bedroom for the first time in many years. Ana clicked off the flashlight and looked up into her mother's eyes.

"This was the secret you mentioned that day down at the creek, isn't it?" Nancy asked.

"Yes, ma'am." Ana nodded.

The two of them stood quietly, staring at each other. Ana figured she was trying to process everything that had happened. "Are you mad that I didn't tell you?"

"I don't know what to say." Ana could tell she was struggling for an answer. "If you had told me back then what you were doing, I probably would have screamed and demanded that you stop. But now...I'm glad you didn't tell me. I think. This is crazy."

"Mom," Ana spoke up. "Maybe life is just crazy sometimes. You trusted me to not do anything stupid, and you gave me the freedom to figure out things on my own. Yes. It was very scary and thinking back, I probably should not have done any of this." By the look on her face, Ana could tell that her mother was struggling with

168

the shocking reality of it all. "But in the end, it all turned out okay, didn't it?"

Nancy glanced down at her and mumbled, "Uh. Yeah. Sure."

Ana suddenly had a brilliant thought. "Mom? Maybe it's like Romans 8:28 in the Bible!"

"Like what?" her mother tried to focus on what Ana had just said. "What do you mean?"

"You know," she smiled. "That God works out everything for the best for those who love Him and do what He wants them to do!" Ana let the truth of God's Word sink in. "How cool is that? God wanted me to find Mr. Griffin's will and I had to keep it all a secret so that His will could be done!"

Nancy hugged her daughter again. "You never cease to amaze me. You know that?" She gazed over Ana's shoulder into Beatrice Griffin's bedroom. "Oh, my! Oh, my!" she shrieked and covered her mouth with her hand. Ana pulled back from her and twirled around.

"Oh, Mom! Oh, Mom!"

It was obvious that the bedroom had not been touched since the day of Beatrice Griffin's death. The bed, though covered with thick dust, looked slept in. Her nightgown was still laying across a chair. Medicine bottles, a dried-out water glass, and other items still stood on the nightstand. Doors to her closets were standing wide open. It was the only room in the mansion that was still intact. Ana knew why.

You couldn't get in here, could you? The doors were locked, and you didn't have the key. I'll bet that drove you crazy. I wonder if you would have finally just broken down the door. Would you have gone that far?

"Ana?" her mother's voice stirred her out of her thoughts. "Are you okay?"

"Uh, huh," she nodded. "Can you believe this? She died years before he did. He left it just the way it was. I am so glad that you're in here with me."

"I wouldn't miss it for the world! So, what do we do now?"

Ana walked toward the huge dresser standing against the wall. "Let's look around and see what we can find."

"I'll take this side," her mother offered. Ana grinned at the excited tone of her voice.

Mom sounds like she's twelve-years-old, too.

Ana was inspecting the casing around the window, when her mother let out a yell.

"Ana!" she cried. "Over here! I found a button hidden in the bottom of the chair-rail next to the bed!" Moving as quickly as she could, Ana went to where her mother was, pulled out her flashlight again and clicked it on.

"Where?" she asked.

"Right there!" Ana shined the light on the spot where her mother was pointing.

"It's a button all right," she agreed. "Let's see what happens when we push it." Ana pressed firmly on the button.

Click!

A large, built-in bookcase maybe three feet wide and as tall as her mother popped away from the wall.

"Oh, goodness!" cried her mother. "It's a hidden door!"

Ana glanced at her mother and thought to herself.

Imagine that.

Keeping the flashlight directed at the opening, Ana walked over and easily pulled the bookcase away from the wall. She looked at her mother. "My turn," she giggled and disappeared into the darkness. "Oh, neat!" Ana cried from inside the wall. "It's a hallway!"

Ana's mother peeked into the opening and could see her daughter several feet away shining the flashlight in every direction. "Oh cool!" Ana shouted, "I've found an elevator!"

"An elevator? Are you sure?"

"Pretty sure," laughed Ana and shined the light toward her mother. "Are you coming?"

"Do you think it's safe?"

"Of course!" declared Ana. "This whole place was built like a fortress."

Nancy tiptoed into the hallway. "Well, this is much larger than I thought it would be," she admitted. The hallway was at least six feet wide.

"They had to be able to get her wheelchair in here and move it around," explained Ana, who had gone past the elevator deeper into the darkness.

"Wheelchair?" asked her mother.

"Yes, ma'am," she added. "Beatrice had cancer. I don't know for how long. But it makes sense that he would build this hallway wide enough for her wheelchair to fit."

Nancy didn't respond and stopped in front of the elevator. "What are you looking for?"

172

Several feet away, Ana had reached the end of the hallway and was busy shining the light up and down, inspecting the corners. "This!" she cried and pushed on the left side of the wall. A door popped open in front of her.

"Oh, my goodness!" squealed her mother and walked toward her. "It's another door! How did you know it was there?" she exited the hallway. Ana and her mother were standing in the back of a huge walk-in closet.

"Now this makes perfect sense!" announced Ana.

"What do you mean?" Her mother was looking around at the men's clothes and other items.

"Simple," she explained. "This closet is in Mr. Griffin's bedroom. This door gave him access to the elevator without having to go through Beatrice's room." She turned and walked back into the hidden hallway. "Come on! Let's check it out!"

Nancy followed her daughter. "Check what out?"

Several feet inside, Ana stopped. "The elevator, of course!" She shined the light on the door in front of her. "This must be how you open it." She pushed the plain-looking, sliding door to the right. "Come on, Mom!" Ana got into the elevator.

"Anastasia Stilwell!" her mother stuck her head through the door. "Do you know what you're doing?"

"Sure! Come on! We've got to see where the elevator goes! Get in!"

Nancy Stilwell bowed her head, even though it wasn't necessary, and stepped into the rather large elevator. Ana shined the flashlight on the wall where she saw a brass plate with two buttons and arrows pointing up and down.

"This looks easy enough." Ana pulled the sliding door shut. She stared at her mother. "I know that Chuck said we shouldn't turn on any lights, until an electrician can check everything out, but I'm dying to see if this works."

"I hope we don't die trying!" exclaimed her mother. "Don't you think we should call Andrew?"

"He wouldn't fit," snickered Ana. "Hang on, Mom! Here goes nothing!" She pushed the button with the arrow pointing down. Without warning and without a sound, they started moving downward.

"We're going to die!" screamed her mother.

"Well, if we do, at least we get to go to heaven and see Jesus...together!" shouted Ana.

"That's not funny," scolded her mother.

"Don't worry, Mom!" Ana laughed. "We're not going to die, because we are almost there."

The elevator stopped smoothly without jolting them at all. "This must be a well-built piece of equipment," remarked Ana. In front of her was a door just like the one on the third floor. "First floor! Everyone out!" she said and pushed the door to the side. The two of them exited out into another hallway. It looked to be the same size as the one upstairs. Ana shined the flashlight toward the left. "Let's see where this goes." Her mother followed close behind. At the end of the hall, Ana recognized immediately the back side of a hinged, paneled door. It reminded her of the one in the rear hallway of the mansion.

"What do we do now?" cried her mother.

Ana didn't answer but pushed on the left side of the panel. It popped open in front of them. She and her mother walked out into the end of the small private dining area on the first floor, where they had been earlier in the day. Ana closed the paneled door behind them. To her right, she found a button in the molding and showed it to her mother.

"Pretty exciting, huh Mom?"

"Exciting is not the word I would use," she took a deep breath. "More like terrifying, if you ask me."

Ana gave her a wide, show-all-your-teeth grin, and they both broke out laughing. They walked together back down the halls to the main room. Andrew jumped to his feet when they entered the room from the carpeted corridor to the right of the staircase.

"How did you two get down here?"

Ana and her mother glanced at each other. "It's a secret!" they said in unison and laughed as they briskly walked past Andrew toward the front door and opened it.

"This is a lot of fun," Nancy put her arm around Ana's shoulder as they skipped down the front steps.

"What do you mean, 'It's a secret?'" Andrew fussed following close behind.

* * * * *

Later that evening Ana was lying on her bed staring at the ceiling—thinking. The door to her room was open and she faintly heard someone coming up the stairs. She could tell it wasn't Connor because he never climbed them slowly, and her father caused them to creak and groan.

"Mom?" Her voice echoed down the upstairs hall. Seconds later her mother stuck her head in the door. In her arms were fresh towels for the upstairs bathroom.

"Did you call me?"

Ana saw the towels. "Those aren't the ones from the mansion, are they?"

"No," she patted them. "These are ours." Ana watched as her mother walked over and placed the stack of towels on the top of her dresser. She took a couple of steps toward Ana's bed and continued, "but I did take a closer look at the things we brought back home with us—I think some of them were never used. I checked online and found out that good quality towels can last up to ten years with normal use. So, once they're washed, we'll be able to tell."

"Oh. That's good," replied Ana half-heartedly. "Mom, I don't really care if they're any good or not. I just know how much you like stuff like that. That's why I wanted you to see them." Ana used her finger to outline the design on the colorful comforter on her bed. Her mother watched her and didn't say anything. After several seconds, Ana spoke up. "Mom? Can we talk?"

"Of course," Nancy Stilwell went over, poked her head out into the hall just to make sure that Connor wasn't lurking about and quietly closed the door. She walked to Ana's bed and sat down on the edge. "So, what do you want to talk about?"

Ana kept tracing the outline of the design on her bed cover. She wasn't smiling. After a while, she stopped and laid on her back.

"Mom, I don't want the money and everything to change our family."

"Oh," said her mother softly, "What do you mean?"

"I've thought about it a lot," she began and then paused. Her mother waited patiently. Ana turned toward her, propping herself up on her elbow. "Mom, I don't want us to move into the mansion. I want us to stay right here—live here—in this house." She gazed at her mother and continued, "I want us to keep on having family movie night in the living room. I want you to pop the popcorn in your favorite pan in our kitchen." Ana turned on her back and gently rubbed her hands back and forth across the bedspread. "And I want to sleep in my bed, in my room." Ana sniffed and wiped her nose on her sleeve. "And even though it sounds completely and utterly crazy, I want to keep on sharing the upstairs bathroom with Connor." Her mother moved closer and leaned over to hug her. Then she let go of Ana and stood up.

"Well, I guess we aren't moving into the mansion, huh?"

"Are you disappointed, Mom?"

"Heavens, no!" she blurted out. "In fact, I'm relieved! That place is gigantic!" She reached out and lovingly took Ana's hands in hers. Leaning in close to her daughter again, she whispered, "and to be perfectly honest, after going through the place and seeing everything today, I have been worried sick all afternoon."

"About what?" Ana shook her head.

"That your brother would end up breaking something valuable."

Ana stuck both hands up into the air. "That's why I make him stay outside or with Andrew whenever he goes over there." She and her mother stared at each other and then burst out laughing. Ana scooted over and they both lay on the bed staring at the ceiling and just listening to each other breathe.

"Thank you for asking me to go with you today. It meant a lot to me."

Ana reached over, found her mother's hand and held on to it. "Thank you. There was no way that I was going into Beatrice Griffin's bedroom without you."

Almost a minute passed before Ana's mother spoke. "You know, your father and I have never asked you about what really happened...about how you found the will. We figured that you would tell us someday, when you're ready."

Ana closed her eyes and sighed, "I can tell you that I did not do anything wrong. I found the key that I used to get in, right where Rudolph Griffin left it." She leaned over and noticed that her mother had tears in her eyes. "Like I told everyone, I can't explain it, but I am positive that Mr. Griffin wanted me to find his will. But there is a reason why I can't tell you about how I found it...not yet." Ana felt the tears coming into her eyes, too. "Mom, I need you and dad to please trust me just a little longer."

"Oh, Ana!" she reached out and put her arm around her daughter. "We trust you, completely! And we are so proud of you."

Chapter Fifteen

Ana forgot to set her alarm and sat straight up. "What on earth is going on?" She grabbed her cell phone on the night-stand next to her bed and checked the time. "Oh, wonderful!" She jumped out of bed, hurried across the hall and pushed open Connor's door. "Come on, sleepy head, wake up! I'll go downstairs and see if breakfast's ready. But if we don't hurry, we'll never make it in time." Her brother moved under his covers and moaned. "Okay!" she turned and stumbled down the hall. "Don't blame me if you have to walk to school."

"Good grief!" she heard Connor complain as she started down the stairs.

"Mom? Dad? Anybody?" she called. No answer.

She walked through the downstairs into the kitchen. Her father was sitting at the breakfast table, hidden behind the morning newspaper and drinking his coffee.

"What are you doing up?" he asked lowering the paper.

"Dad! It's Friday!" she rolled her eyes at him. "Uh? School?"

He put the paper back up in front of his face. "Uh? Teacher's Workday? Uh? No school today. Remember?"

Ana slumped down in a chair, leaned over, rested her head on the table, and groaned. "Oh, no."

Connor ambled into the kitchen rubbing his eyes. "Hey! Why didn't you guys wake me up?"

Ana didn't raise her head from the table. "Teacher's Workday. Remember? We've got the day off."

"Are you serious?" he cried. "Yippee!" He spun around and raced back upstairs. "Look out bed, here I come!"

Ana's mother entered the kitchen from the back porch. "Good morning, honey. What are you doing up? Today's Teacher's Workday at your school, so you've got the day off. Didn't you remember?"

"No, ma'am," she moaned. "I'm going back to bed."

"I'll come get you and Connor in about an hour, when breakfast is ready."

"Sounds like a plan," she yawned and staggered out of the kitchen. Out in the hall she ran into Andrew, who was heading toward his first cup of coffee.

"Good morning," he muttered. Ana could tell something was wrong.

"What's eating you?" she asked. He glared at her.

"I don't mean to spoil your fun, but I need to know how you two were able to get back downstairs yesterday without me seeing you?" Ana could tell that he was not smiling nor kidding. "Is there another staircase in the mansion that I don't know about?"

Ana shook her head. "We found an elevator."

"An elevator? Are you serious?"

"Uh, huh," she yawned again. "We rode it from the third floor down to the first."

"Does it stop on all three floors?" he asked.

"Nope. Just the first and the third. It connects the upstairs bedroom with the private family dining room."

"Imagine that," he muttered and scratched the side of his head.

"Yep." Ana started up the stairs, anxious to see if she could go back to sleep.

"Since you don't have school this morning, could we ride over there, and you show me where it is?" he asked.

"Sounds like...a plan," she said sleepily.

* * * * *

After breakfast she and Andrew drove over to the mansion. Connor was still in his bed or was busy in his room, so they were able to get away without causing a scene. Neither spoke as they rode along. Soon they were making their way through the mansion toward the family dining room at the rear of the building.

Ana showed Andrew the button hidden in the molding of the chair rail.

"How in the world did you ever find this?"

"Seriously?" she grinned at him and pulled out her flashlight.

"Sorry, ma'am. I forgot who I was talking to," he shook his head.

Ana pulled on the hidden panel door in the wall, clicked on her flashlight and walked into the dark hallway. "Are you coming?" she called.

"Will I fit?" he stuck his head inside.

"Barely!" she laughed.

Andrew ducked his head and squeezed through the opening. "I hate being in tight places where I can't move around."

"Well, you're the one who wanted to see the elevator," Ana shined the flashlight. "So, here it is!"

Andrew slowly stood up straight and was glad that he didn't bump his head on the ceiling. "And you said it goes up to the third floor but doesn't stop on the second?"

"You got it," she nodded. "But I suggest that we not try riding it. Mom and I took a chance that it would work yesterday, but I don't want to push it."

"Are you afraid we might get stuck?"

"No. I don't want Chuck to get mad that we used the electricity before everything is checked out."

"Gotcha, uh, yes ma'am," agreed Andrew.

Ana shined her flashlight at the end of the hallway. "You have got to be kidding me!" she exclaimed.

Andrew almost jumped out of his skin. "What now?"

"It's another door," she said. It was about fifteen feet away from the elevator. "I guess I was so excited about getting out yesterday, that I simply forgot to check out the other end of the hall."

Ana scrutinized every inch of the massive wooden door with her flashlight and recognized immediately the shape of the keyhole. She rubbed the outside of her jeans pocket and felt the outline of the skeleton key.

If this fits it will be a miracle...or maybe not.

Andrew reached out and tried the latch handle. "It's locked."

Ana took out the key and inserted it into the hole. "Let's see if this works," she smiled and turned it to the left.

Click!

"You've got a key?" he cried.

"It's my mansion," she glanced up at him, snickered, and opened the door.

There was a landing on the other side with stone steps leading downward and another door to the right. Ana examined this door. It had a dead bolt with normal-looking key

186

sticking in the lock. She turned the dead bolt, unlocked the door and opened it. Walking through, she immediately knew that they were in a rear hallway of the mansion. Ana turned around and looked at Andrew, who was right behind her.

"We're close to the kitchen." She walked back through the door to the top of the landing and pointed down the steps. "I wonder what's down there?" She glanced up at him. "You with me?"

"Oh, yes ma'am. All the way!"

Slowly they began descending the steep steps that curved to the right. At the bottom, she heard Andrew let out a deep sigh as she shined her flashlight around in the darkness.

"Looks like a huge cellar," he remarked. They started at the right and went around the room. The walls were lined on three sides with built-in shelves. Some were almost empty. Other shelves had cans, jars, and boxes still stacked neatly in rows. Dust covered everything. In one corner stood cases of soft drinks and bottled water. Ana could tell that they had not been moved or touched for years. She walked over and removed one of the boxes of cake mix, turned it over and checked the date. 11:04:98.

This was bought just months before you died.

She replaced the box and thought about Lawrence Hill.

You never made it down here, did you? The door to the cellar was bolted shut, and you didn't have the key because Rudolph Griffin left it sticking in the lock.

Andrew said something, but Ana wasn't listening. She was too busy studying the built-in shelves on the far end wall ...and thinking.

We've got to be almost directly under the rear terrace on the back side of the mansion. One of these shelves should be hiding the entrance to the other tunnel. The question is, 'Which one?'

"Are you ready to go?" repeated Andrew, stirring Ana out of her thoughts.

Ana sighed, checked the time on her cell phone and nodded. "Mom should have lunch ready when we get back." They climbed back up the steps. Ana took the skeleton key out of her pocket and inserted it into the lock of the massive wooden door that led to the elevator hallway.

"Why are you locking it?" asked Andrew.

"I don't want anyone to know about the elevator except you, me, Mom, Dad, and Chuck, of course."

"That's not a bad idea."

"I thought you might like it," she smiled and opened the door to the rear hallway near the kitchen. To the left, she saw a door that led outside.

I'll bet that's the one Lawrence Hill came in through. We'll need to get the lock changed.

She turned the dead bolt, locked the door to the cellar, pulled out the key, and stuck it in her pocket. The two of them started down the hall. As they turned the corner that led to the main entrance hall, Ana abruptly halted in her tracks.

"We need to go back and shut the hidden panel door in the family dining room!"

"Good thinking," agreed Andrew.

"I'm learning," smiled Ana.

* * * * *

After lunch, Chuck arrived for their regular Friday afternoon business meeting. Ana learned that her fortune had grown again— more dividend statements had arrived from other stocks she owned. Everything else was about the same as always, except that Chuck did mention that he was concerned about a call he had received from a contact in one of the companies she controlled. He wasn't prepared to go into details, he said, but that he would keep her informed.

"Oh," he added as he walked toward the front door, "don't forget to pick up the floral arrangements today. Here's the address." He handed Ana a card.

"*Thinking of You Florist Shop?*" she grinned. "Sounds... precious."

"Rachel Bennett is the owner. She is very talented... and a dear friend," Chuck raised his eyebrows and nodded with his head. Andrew walked up behind Ana. She handed him the card.

"We need to pick up the flowers for the Griffins' graves," she told him. Then she turned and looked at Chuck.

"And we'll behave at the florist shop," she grinned, "I promise."

* * * * *

Ana was looking forward to picking up the flowers. When they arrived, there was no bell to announce them, like one would expect, so they entered without being noticed.

"Looks like she's busy with someone," Ana whispered. "Let's stand over there and wait until she's finished." She motioned to a spot some distance away behind a rather large floor arrangement, like one you might see at a funeral.

They soon learned that the customer was Bertha Claxton, who came in once a year to get birthday flowers for her sister. By the sound of the shop owner's voice, Ana could tell that Bertha was being... difficult.

Andrew leaned down. "Aren't we being sneaky?" His voice was barely audible.

Ana put her finger over her lips and shook her head. "We're being polite," she quietly explained and continued staring through the leaves of the floral creations in front of them. After a few seconds, she glanced up at him and rolled her eyes. "And sneaky."

Bertha Claxton's displeasure suddenly gained in intensity. Ana saw her move her head from side to side, as if she were examining the most important purchase of her seventy-eight years.

"No. It still doesn't look quite right. Something's missing."

"Well, if we put...," Rachel Bennett selected and held a group of extra, different flowers in one hand and began carefully inserting them at random, "this one here, and then one here, and here," she moved around the arrangement as if she were dancing, "and one here, and... here." She finished, wiped her forehead with the sleeve of her shirt and managed a smile. "How's that?"

"Well, I have to admit. That is better." Bertha framed the small arrangement with her ancient hands. "It does add that extra touch, doesn't it?"

"I think so," the patient florist concurred. Ana and Andrew looked at each other, rolled their eyes, and almost broke out laughing.

"This is like watching an old television show," Ana covered her mouth to keep her whisper from coming out as a squeak.

Bertha took a couple of steps back from the counter and then opened her eyes wide and glared at the flower artist. "But the question is: How much more will that cost?" As she walked back toward the counter, she lowered her head, opened her purse, and pulled out her wallet. She began fingering through the bills inside, counting them. Rachel Bennett moved over to check a list of flowers and prices to her right. Ana could clearly see her face and could tell that she was trying hard to keep her growing frustration under control.

"Those will add... three dollars and twenty-five cents," she stated.

Bertha peered over the top of her glasses that had slid down to the end of her nose. She clamped her right hand over her wallet and demanded, "So how much are we talking about in all?"

Rachel examined the small arrangement in front of her, "That comes to $21 dollars, plus tax, of course."

"Twenty-one dollars? No. No. That's too much," Bertha raised her skinny hand in front of the florist. "My birthday present from my sister cost twenty dollars, because that's what we agreed to spend on each other this year. Twenty dollars, plus tax of course, but not a penny more. My sister will want to see the receipt."

Ana watched and thought back to the way her life used to be.

Before, twenty dollars would have sounded like a lot of money. I would have had to save up for months from my allowance to have that much.

She remembered using her left-over birthday money to purchase a stuffed toy turtle and a flashlight. That seemed like ages ago. Now, she and Andrew were about to pick up three gorgeous arrangements that cost over two-hundred dollars apiece. Six-hundred dollars every other week—for flowers! Ana smiled. She didn't have to worry about having enough money in her pocket to pay for them. Not anymore. Chuck would take care of the bill. She wondered if she would have to personally pay for anything ever again. The scene taking place in front of her drew Ana out of her daydream.

"Well we could remove a couple of these." The florist carefully plucked out two of the added flowers from what would be the back of the arrangement, "There. Now it costs twenty dollars exactly, uh, plus tax." She proudly held up the finished work. "How's that look?"

"Well, I don't know," replied Bertha. She lightly bit the finger of her right hand, while twisting her head to the left. After pulling the finger out of her mouth, she pointed at the flowers. "Now, it looks lopsided! No. That won't work. Can't you fix it?"

Rachel Bennett yanked all the flowers out of the cheap, plastic vase and dropped them on the counter. Andrew suddenly coughed and her head popped up. Ana poked her bodyguard in the side and the two of them moved to where the shop owner could see them.

"Oh, my goodness!" Rachel exclaimed. "Excuse me, Mrs. Claxton, I'll be right back. Let me take care of these other customers. They're here to pick up an order. It will only take a minute."

"But I was here first," Bertha complained. "How long is it going to take?"

The florist ignored her and disappeared through a door into the rear of her shop. After a minute she reemerged carrying one of the arrangements. A young female assistant behind her was carrying the other two. They were safely packaged in large boxes, so they wouldn't be damaged while being transported. A large, clear plastic window on the front of each box allowed the arrangement inside to be viewed without being opened.

"Here they are," Rachel beamed as she walked to the end of the long work counter as far away from Bertha Claxton as possible. She carefully set her box down and took the others from her assistant until all three were standing on the counter together. Ana could tell they weren't heavy, just big. "Are these all right?"

"They are gorgeous, Mrs. Bennett," approved Ana. Andrew reached down and gently picked up two of the large boxes. Ana got the last one. They turned and started to leave. The shop owner hurried over to open the door and then held it for them to walk through. "Thank you so much, Mrs. Bennett," smiled Ana. "See you in two weeks."

"Yes, ma'am. Thank you! Thank you so much! Have a nice day."

Ana looked in her direction, blinked her eyes, and grinned, "I hope you'll be able to have a nice day, too."

The kind florist made a face, and they both laughed. She turned and walked back into the shop as the door automatically, slowly closed. Ana could hear the loud voice of the older customer from outside the store. Bertha Claxton's curiosity had reached the boiling point.

"Well, who in the world was that little girl?" she demanded to know, "and that huge man with her? You just let them waltz in here, pick up all those flowers and waltz back out without paying for them. Who in the world does she think she is?"

Ana stopped and gazed up at Andrew. "Wait a minute, I want to hear what she says." She saw Rachel Bennett put her hands on her hips and glare at the elderly customer.

"Hush! Be quiet!" She motioned toward the door. "That's Ana Stilwell and her bodyguard, Andrew! They just picked up six-hundred dollars-worth of flowers. Six hundred dollars! And it's a standing order for every two weeks—every Friday from now on! She puts them on the graves of the Griffins." The store owner glanced back toward the front door and could see that Ana and Andrew were still standing just outside. "She probably heard you!"

All the color drained out of Bertha Claxton's wrinkled, old face. She leaned over on the counter. "I feel sick," she whined. The flowers for her pitiful little birthday gift were just inches from her nose. She reached down and picked up one of the brochures advertising the "Thinking About You" Florist Shop and fanned herself with it. "She must think I'm a complete idiot."

Rachel Bennett didn't offer her opinion on that subject, but instead, walked over and picked up the hand-full of flowers lying on the counter.

"Okay, Let's see what we can put together for twenty dollars...plus tax."

Chapter Sixteen

When they got to the parking lot at the rear of the mansion, Ana jumped out, walked to the edge of the lawn and said excitedly, "Oh, look!" She pointed at the cleaned and trimmed, white crushed-stone walkway that led to the rear terrace. "We won't have to track through the wet grass anymore."

"Well, that's good news," remarked Andrew as he opened the left rear door of the Mercedes and gingerly began removing the large boxes. He set them one after the other on the pavement.

"Can you help me here, please?" he had picked up his two boxes and was standing there, waiting for Ana to come get the last one.

"Oh, sure." She hurried over, bent down and picked it up. "I guess we'll have to get used to doing this, huh?"

Without saying a word, they made their way down the cleared path to the rear terrace. Turning left, they walked straight away from the mansion toward the mausoleum. At the massive green copper door, they helped each other place the floral boxes on the marble floor. Ana watched as Andrew took hold of the long lever with both hands, shoved it up and to the left. The hinges groaned as he pulled it open. "I'll need to remember to bring some oil the next time we come."

The weather was clear, and the sun was shining as they entered the mausoleum.

"Oh, goodness! Look!" cried Ana.

"Unbelievable," whispered Andrew from behind her.

The brilliant display of colors reflecting off the white marble walls and tombs was breathtaking. "I don't think I've ever seen anything this beautiful in all my life!" she said reverently.

"Me, neither," he agreed. They placed the boxes next to Lewis Griffin's tomb. Ana bowed her head, reached out and rested her hand on the cold marble. Andrew bowed his head, too.

"Dear Lord," she prayed softly, her young voice echoing in the silence, "please help me to always care about and honor the memory of this family. Amen."

"Amen," added Andrew reverently.

"Let's do Lewis' grave first, then Beatrice's and then Mr. Griffin's last," instructed Ana. She looked through the clear window in the floral boxes and found the one with his name. Andrew reached up and removed the gorgeous, empty crystal vase from the top of the tomb. He walked over to the sink, filled it with fresh water, brought it back and set it on the floor. In the meantime, Ana had opened the large box and carefully removed the flowers. Their timing was perfect, and she placed them in the vase. There was a string holding the arrangement together.

"Let me take care of that," offered Andrew. He pulled out a small pocket-knife and cut the string. The flowers fell into place.

"Now, that's beautiful!" pronounced Ana. She made sure the white ribbon with Lewis' name was visible. "These flowers are perfect. I love it that they don't need fluffing or fixing." She glanced up at Andrew. "What do you think?"

"I think you are an amazing young lady."

"Thank you," she smiled without looking up. Ana reached down and firmly grabbed one side of the vase. "Ready?"

"Ready," replied Andrew and took hold of it with her. Together they lifted the vase and placed it on top of the marble vault. Ana gently rubbed her hand across the smooth, cold surface again and patted it softly. Then she turned and gazed at her bodyguard.

"They would want us to honor him first," she explained. Andrew didn't say anything. After a brief pause, they turned and began the process all over again for Beatrice's grave. Ana stood back to make sure the flowers were in the exact middle of her tomb.

"She was a very beautiful and graceful lady," she explained. "The people of this town loved her very much." As she stood there quietly, Ana remembered the newspaper article about her funeral and thought about Rudolph Griffin.

You stood right here, didn't you?

After a moment, she added, "He had a hard time dealing with her death." Andrew stood quietly at attention.

Rudolph Griffin's grave was last. They repeated the steps as before without a word. After straightening out his ribbon, Ana reached down to take hold of the vase of flowers. Andrew was only a split second behind her but was too late. Ana sneezed and her sudden hand movement to cover her mouth knocked over the vase. Andrew tried to grab it but missed.

"Oh no!" she screamed. The flowers scattered on the floor. The water sloshed out and up against the base of the tomb. "What a mess! What a horrible mess!" she cried and sneezed again. She stared at Andrew with her hand over her mouth. "What do we do?"

"There's a roll of paper towels in the trunk of the car. I'll run and get them!" Ana sneezed again. "I'll be right back. You wait here." Andrew turned and raced out the door of the mausoleum.

"Thank you," she called and added, "You don't have to run. We've got plenty of time." Andrew ignored her suggestion. Ana went to the door and watched him jog back toward the car that was parked near the mansion. Then she turned around and walked back over to Griffin's tomb to inspect her mess.

Huh?

The spilled water from the vase was gone. Ana stared in disbelief, quickly dropped to her knees and felt the floor with her hand. It was barely wet.

Where did the water go?

She stood back up just as Andrew arrived with a roll of paper towels. He was breathing heavily. Ana turned around, held out her arms and stared at him.

202

"The water's gone!"

"What do you mean? That's impossible!" He yanked off several sheets, pushed past her, and got down on his hands and knees. He moved the spilled flowers to the side out of the way and began wiping the floor with the towels. "Oh, my goodness. You're right! The floor's just a little damp. What's going on? The water couldn't have just disappeared!" He bent down closer, studying where the floor met the edge of the tomb. "Okay, okay," he pointed. "There's a crack in the joint. That's where the water went."

Ana sighed. "Oh, well. It doesn't matter now. The main thing is that we can clean it all up. At least I didn't smash the vase to pieces. Is it cracked at all?"

Andrew picked it up and examined it. "It looks all right to me. I'll go fill it up with water again and see if it leaks."

"And I'll pick up the flowers."

"Sounds like a plan," grinned Andrew.

"Please," groaned Ana.

Soon the vase with the floral arrangement was ready to be placed on the tomb again. Andrew glanced down at her and asked, "Want me to do it?"

"That's probably not a bad idea," she admitted, still a bit upset that she had caused the accident. When they were finished, Ana stepped back and admired the scene.

"I just want to make sure that you can see the white ribbons with their names," she explained. "Even though we are the only ones who will ever see them, it still matters to me." The two of them stood silently for a couple of minutes. "Andrew, thank you for being here with me," she whispered softly, "I could never do this without you."

"It's an honor and a privilege, Miss Stilwell."

Ana touched him lightly on his arm. "Please call me, Ana. And please cool it with the 'ma'am' stuff. It makes me feel old."

"I do it out of respect," he said and stood up straight. "I work for you and I enjoy showing you the respect you deserve. You are making a difference in the lives of so many people. I'm proud of you and I want others to respect you, too."

"Gotcha," she nodded.

They stood there for a moment. Ana pulled out her cell phone and took a couple of photos of the inside. "Mom will want to see these," she said. They picked up the empty boxes and paper towels and exited the mausoleum.

204

Andrew pushed the massive door shut and turned the latch to seal it. Ana looked at the boxes. "These are still in pretty good shape. We ought to ask Mrs. Bennett if she wants to reuse them."

Andrew shook his head. "You just spent $600 on three flower arrangements. I'm sure the boxes are included."

Ana frowned, "I just don't like to waste the money, if I don't have to."

After a few steps, Andrew stopped and looked at her. "Please forgive me for what I said. If you want to take these boxes back to the florist shop, I would be honored to drive you there."

"Thank you," she said.

When they got to the rear terrace, Ana thought about the cellar beneath them and stopped. She turned around and looked back at the mausoleum.

"Did you forget something?" asked Andrew.

"No," she shook her head and they continued walking toward the car. "Just thinking."

* * * * *

That evening, Ana walked into the kitchen and covered her mouth to keep from laughing out loud. Andrew was hulking behind her mother.

He must have sensed her presence, because he turned toward her and placed his huge index finger across his poked-out lips—the international sign to be quiet. He and her mother were listening for the single kernel of popcorn sizzling in the pan to pop. Ana went straight to the cabinet where the bowls were stored. As she opened the door, she chuckled. The plastic bowls now had names on them— crudely written in black permanent marker. Ana recognized her brother's handwriting.

This looks like Connor's handiwork.

As she set them out on the table, her mother began vigorously shaking the popcorn pan while holding the top with her other hand.

"She is really good at this!" exclaimed Andrew. For security reasons, he randomly rotated his weekly night off. Oddly enough, even though he had been staying in the house since right after Ana inherited the Griffin fortune, this was his first time to experience "family night and a movie" at the Stilwell's.

"Popcorn's ready!" shouted Ana's mother. "Get it while it's hot!"

"Coming!" Ana heard her father and brother call from the living room. They had been arranging the furniture and getting the movie ready.

Nancy glanced at Andrew, "Go get your bowl!" she ordered. He spun around and looked at Ana and raised his hands, signaling he needed help. Ana pointed at the large blue one with his name on it.

"You mean I have my own bowl?" he beamed.

"You are now officially a Stilwell," she proudly proclaimed.

Andrew held out his bowl as her mother filled it with the delicious treat.

"Do you have any sug...?" He didn't get to finish, because Ana was violently shaking her head NO and, at the same time, making a cutting motion across her throat with her finger.

"Salt! The salt is over here, Andrew," Ana blurted out and pointed. Her mother was busy filling bowls for Connor and Ana's father. Andrew walked over to Ana several feet away.

"I like to put sugar on my popcorn," he whispered in her ear.

"Not in this house," she corrected. "Mom's a purist. She allows us to put salt and maybe cheese sprinkles on it but thinks sugar on popcorn is an abomination."

"Oh," he stuttered. "Okay. I'll try a little salt and lots of cheese sprinkles."

Ana laughed. "Wise choice."

* * * * *

Soon everyone was seated in the living room with filled popcorn bowls and something to drink. Ana's father stood up in front of the television screen. It was his night to pick the film. She could tell he was getting ready to announce the title.

"Instead of going to the Rent-a-Movie Box tonight, on the way home from work I stopped off at the library." Ana sat up in her seat and gazed intently at him. "They've got a huge selection of DVDs and Blue Rays. So, I checked one out. It's a classic!" he beamed.

"Oh no!" growled Connor. "That means it's a black and white cowboy movie!"

"No," he glared at his almost nine-year old son. "It is not a cowboy movie. And it is not black and white." He looked around the room and then directly at Ana. "I remembered you asking questions about Germany and World War II some time ago, so I decided that we would watch—drumroll please—*The Great Escape!*" He held the cover up and moved it back and forth for all to see. Then he looked at it again himself. "It's one of my favorites and it's got a

208

lot of famous stars in it: Steve McQueen, James Garner, and Charles Bronson!"

"Never heard of them!" grumbled Ana's younger brother.

"Quiet. Eat some popcorn," suggested her mother.

"What's it about?" Ana tried to act like she was interested.

"Oh, well. Uh. It's about a bunch of soldiers trying to escape from a German prisoner-of-war camp. It's really exciting." He surveyed the faces in the room. "Anyway, it's my night to choose and I choose this." He held up the movie cover again.

"I want to see it!" exclaimed Andrew.

"Me, too," added Ana.

"Great! I think you'll love it. It's one of my favorites."

"You've already told us that, dear," reminded Ana's mother.

"Well, it is!" Ronnie Stilwell turned off the lights, took his seat, and started the film with the remote. Connor slouched in his chair. Ana's mother put her hand over his mouth to stifle his comments. Before long, however, he quit pouting and acted like he was interested in the movie.

Ana liked it because it was about Germany. She remembered the German words on the bottom of the crystal vase she'd found. When the prisoners started talking about digging a tunnel, she got really interested. Their plan was to get over one hundred prisoners out at once. The tunnel entrance was concealed underneath a very hot stove in the barracks. They used two bed slats with grooves cut out as handles on either side of the stove to pick it up and move it. Then they pried up a large piece of tile flooring to reveal the trap door.

That is so cool.

In a crucial scene of the movie, the German guards made all the prisoners leave the barracks. One of them saw a metal coffee pot on the stove and picked it up to pour himself a cup. It was so hot he dropped it on the floor. The top came off and coffee spilled out at the base of the stove. But instead of making a brown puddle, the coffee instantly disappeared beneath the tile. Ana sat straight up.

Oh, my goodness. It's like the spilled flower water in the mausoleum!

Ana froze in her seat with her eyes glued to the screen. She watched as the German guard in the movie shouted, and more guards rushed in. They moved the stove, pried up the tile, and discovered the hidden escape tunnel.

Is there a hole underneath Rudolph Griffin's tomb?

Suddenly, another thought hit her.

I wonder if Andrew saw it. Is he wondering the same thing I am?

Slowly, she cut her eyes to the right and then let out a sigh of relief. Her huge bodyguard was busy eating popcorn and trading elbow shots with Connor. She smiled and returned to watching the film. Later, when the prisoners began digging another tunnel, the question from minutes before resurfaced.

Where did the flower water go?

Chapter Seventeen

The screeching tires of a truck in front of her house woke Ana out of a very deep sleep. She sat straight up in bed but wasn't curious about the cause of the noise. She was just thankful to be rescued out of the nightmare she had been having, in which she was trapped inside the mausoleum.

"Praise the Lord that's over!" she exhaled. She checked the time on her cell phone.

6:45 a.m.

I wonder if Dad's already up.

Ana slipped on her goofy-looking house shoes and quietly made her way downstairs. Her dad was an early riser and she knew where he would be—sitting in his favorite chair at the kitchen table. Ana peeked around the corner and smiled.

He loves this time of the morning, where he can be alone, drink his coffee, pray, read the Bible... and the newspaper.

She tiptoed back down the hall toward Andrew's room, hoping the door was closed. It was. Ana leaned as closely as possible without touching it and listened. The deep, raspy sound of his snoring made her snicker.

It will take more than screeching tires to wake him up.

Back in her room she crawled into bed and just laid there, staring at the ceiling and thinking. She remembered the scene from the movie the night before and shook her head.

Why would there be an opening underneath Mr. Griffin's tomb? That doesn't make any sense.

After going over everything that had happened the previous day, another thought popped into her mind.

It had to be Rudolph Griffin that bolted and locked the door from the elevator hallway to the hall by the kitchen. That way, he had access from his room, down the elevator, to the kitchen, or the cellar, or to the rear hallway and an outside door.

She leaned over in her bed and saw the door to her closet.

But why was that cellar door locked from the inside?

Ana got up out of bed, walked over to her desk, sat down and took out a blank piece of paper. Using a pencil, she began to sketch a rough outline of the outside walls of the mansion from memory. Then she added the secret tunnels and doors. When she finished, Ana put the pencil sideways in her mouth, holding it tightly with her teeth. Unconsciously making a series of small bite marks in the soft wood, she carefully examined her artwork. Grabbing the pencil out of her mouth, she added the outline of the cellar on the backside of the mansion. Ana tapped the pencil on her drawing.

I've got to find out if there is an entrance to the other end of that closed off tunnel from the cellar.

She got dressed in her play clothes. Folding up the drawing small enough to fit in her back pocket, Ana grabbed her flashlight and her cell phone. Like a slinking cat, she crept silently downstairs, careful not to wake Connor, or Andrew. It was 7:22 a.m. when she strolled into the kitchen.

"I thought all almost-teenagers slept in on Saturdays," her father teased without lowering his newspaper.

Ana walked over and hugged him around his neck. "Well, good morning to you, too!" Her father lowered his paper and leaned into her hug. "I'm going to make me a jam sandwich for breakfast, if that's okay?" She let him go, disappeared into the pantry and re-emerged later with a loaf of bread.

"What are you going to *jam* in the middle this time?" he chuckled.

"A piece of cheese, if we still have some." Ana put two pieces of whole wheat sandwich bread on a paper towel and got the sliced cheese out of the refrigerator. Then she jammed them together and held it up in the air. "See, a cheese, uh, jam sandwich."

"I think you are supposed to use jelly or jam." Her father quipped, turning the newspaper to a new page.

"Well, today, it's cheese," she announced and headed toward the back door. "Dad, would you please tell Andrew that I'm down at the creek, if he asks?"

"You haven't been to your favorite spot for some time, have you?"

"Uh, no sir. I haven't," she grabbed her jacket and put it on. "I'd just like to be by myself for a while this morning, if that's okay?"

"I'll tell him when he wakes up," said her father. "And I'll let your mother know that you've already had breakfast." Ana walked over, waited for him to put down his coffee cup, and hugged him again around his neck.

"Thanks, Dad!"

"Be careful," he said softly and then added, "do you have your whistle with you, just in case?" Ana pulled on the string around her neck and wiggled the whistle in the air. "Andrew will want to know that you have it." She saw the expression on his face turn serious. "You do know that we love you and are extremely proud of you, right?"

"Yes, sir. I love you, too, Dad." She hugged him again, turned and headed out the door. She made her way down the back stairs and across the yard. When she got to the path heading to the creek, she began cramming the cheese sandwich into her mouth.

I've got maybe one hour before I need to be back. I hope Andrew doesn't come looking for me.

Ana began making her way down the creek. It felt good jumping from rock to rock again, but totally different now. When she saw the stone wall in the distance, she paused.

Oh, that wall over there? Uh, it belongs to me!

At the huge boulder, she stuck her hand into the crevice and pulled down on the lever.

Ker-clunk!

The hidden entrance popped open and Ana crawled inside. She clicked on her flashlight and checked the time.

I've got to hurry.

Minutes later she entered the large room and shined the light on the etching of a man's profile made years before by Rudolph Griffin.

"Did you miss me?" she laughed and then shouted. "I'm so glad that I don't have to whisper anymore!" She turned down the tunnel to the right, passing the odd drawings and the hidden letters that spelled RICKY, always careful to pace off and number her steps. She finally reached the large, metal plate at the end of the tunnel.

"Perfect. Just like I thought. I've got to be standing under the rear corner of the mansion." She knocked on the metal plate with her knuckles, like she was knocking on a door. "Oh, wow! It sounds hollow on the other side. Why didn't I think to do that before?"

She turned, quickly retraced her steps to the large room, and entered the tunnel in the middle. At the massive wooden door, she used her skeleton key to unlock it, walked through, and locked it behind her. Ana sprinted up the steps, down the secret passageway, and pushed open the secret panel door that gave her access into the rear hallway.

"Hello!" she called. Her voice echoed through the mansion. Ana laughed. "Is anyone home?" She stepped out into the hallway and closed the door behind her. As she hurried along toward the rear of the house, Ana chuckled.

If someone had answered me, I would have wet my ever-loving pants for sure!

She made her way to the locked cellar door near the kitchen. Ana used the key Rudolph Griffin had left sticking in it to unlock the dead bolt.

"Okay," she licked her lips. "Let's see what we can find down in the cellar."

Ana clicked on her flashlight and carefully made her way down the curving stone steps. At the bottom, she immediately went to the opposite end of the room and surveyed the scene in front of her. Carefully, she began pulling and pushing on the shelves that were almost empty. She knew how Rudolph Griffin liked to hide things.

"It's got to be one of these, if it's here at all," she reasoned. "Where is it?" she fussed and

218

wiped her forehead on her sleeve. "The other tunnel at the corner of the mansion was pointing in this direction. The entrance has got to be here somewhere!" She finished with the last shelf on the end wall. "Well, that didn't work." Ana turned her gaze to the wall on her left. It was the longest wall in the cellar with shelves from the floor to the ceiling and ran parallel to the rear wall of the mansion. "Okay. You're next!"

She began working her way down it, avoiding shelves stacked with items. Every time she grabbed a shelf, before she began pulling and pushing on it, Ana would say, "Come on! Be the one! Be the one!" When she got to the shelf that was exactly in the middle of the wall, she grabbed it and said it again. "Come on! Be the one! Be the one!"

It was.

"Oh, my goodness!" she screamed. When she pulled on it, the whole shelf popped and folded in on itself, like an accordion. Ana pushed on it and it closed back in place. She pulled on the middle board again and it opened. "This is the coolest thing ever!"

Ana stuck her head through the opening and shined her flashlight around. "It's another room!" she squealed. Once inside she could tell that this room had also been dug by hand, but that it was different from the large room in the other tunnel. To the left against the wall were two large, free-standing lockers. Ana walked over and opened one of them. Several pairs of men's work overalls and pants were hanging on hooks. In the bottom were three pairs of work boots. In another locker were shelves with socks, boots, belts, a hard hat with a light on the front like a miner would wear, and other pieces of work clothes. All were stained and worn from heavy use.

To the right of the lockers was a very simple, uncomfortable-looking bed. Past the bed, on the wall was a large sink and a faucet. Towels were stacked on the shelf above it. Shining the light back at the lockers, she discovered to the left of them a small wooden desk and chair. An old oil lamp was on the desk. Ana imagined Rudolph Griffin sitting there, silhouetted against the flickering light from the lamp. Past the desk she found several shovels, picks, metal rakes, and a couple of long heavy-looking iron rods with chisel points on them leaning against the wall. Beside them was a long wooden box. Next to that on a simple table were two chain saws.

This must have been your base of operations while you worked on the tunnels.

Swinging the light back around to the right, past the lockers, bed and sink, Ana found another wooden door. It was on the wall directly across from the secret shelf door that had allowed her access into the room, so it wasn't the one she was looking for—the one she had to find. Ana continued shining the light around the room.

"There you are!" she cried. A narrow, open tunnel led away from the far end of the room to her right. "I'll bet that's how you got to the other tunnels. This is all coming together now!" Ana moved quickly to the opening and shined her light into the darkness.

"I've got to know," she said and entered the tunnel. It didn't take long before she arrived at the metal door. "I knew it! I knew it!" she exclaimed. There was a serious-looking latch with a large, round knob on her side of the door. After closer examination, she noticed a curving arrow on it.

This looks simple enough.

Holding the flashlight in her mouth, Ana firmly grabbed the knob and turned it to the right.

Screech-Clunk!

The hinges creaked as Ana pushed on the door with all her might to force it open. Removing the flashlight from her mouth, she slowly, she peeked around the edge. "Hallelujah! I knew it! I'm in the tunnel that leads to the large room!"

She glanced up at the ceiling. "And I'm right underneath the corner of the mansion." Ana looked back at the metal door frame. "Boy! Once, you shut this baby behind you that's it!" She left the door standing open, walked back through, and retraced her steps down the tunnel. She thought about Rudolph Griffin.

Why would you need such a serious, one-way door?

Back in the work room, she shined her light back around and stopped at the long wooden box next to the chain saws.

I wonder, what's in there?

Holding the flashlight in her mouth again, she reached down and opened the lid.

"What in the world?" she garbled pass the flashlight. Ana reached down and picked up a small, slender, round, metal container with a valve and breathing mask attached. It reminded her of something a scuba diver might wear, except that it was much smaller. Ana lifted it out of the box. It wasn't heavy at all. "I'll bet you kept this with you whenever you were digging in case the tunnel caved in on you." She carefully replaced the air tank and closed the lid.

Standing back up, she continued scanning the room and on the other door. Ana walked and examined the latch and immediately recognized the shape of the hole in the lock. "Well, hello there! I've seen this before! Let's see if my trusty old skeleton key fits you, too?" Ana pulled out her key, stuck it in the lock and turned it to the left.

Click!

Ana laughed, "Wow! This gets really easy, once you have the key and know what you're doing!" She opened the door and shined her flashlight into more darkness. "Okay," she sighed. "Let's see where this one goes."

After a few steps, she stopped. Ana remembered that she had folded up the paper with her drawing of the mansion and stuck it in her back pants pocket. "Why don't I check my map?"

Holding the paper out in front of her, Ana saw where she had penciled in the cellar. "Okay," she used her finger. "The room has to be on this side of the mansion, because it's on this wall of the cellar. Wow! It's directly beneath the rear terrace." Ana shined the light on her drawing, then at the tunnel in front of her, and back at the drawing.

"Dear Lord Jesus, please help me!" she slowly walked farther and farther into the darkness. Ana was shaking all over. She wadded up the drawing and crammed it into her pocket. In the distance she began to make out the shape of something. "What is that?" she wondered. "What on earth is that?"

Finally, Ana knew what it was and gasped. In front of her, resting on a kind of metal and wood contraption was an impressive, stainless-steel casket. Holding the flashlight in her shaking right hand, she slowly made her way closer and closer until she was standing right beside it. Ana clenched her teeth and examined the top. It was wet.

"Oh, my dear Lord Jesus, please help me!" Ana cried and immediately clamped her hand over her mouth to stifle her scream. She rubbed the surface just to make sure. "It's the water from the flowers! It's got to be!" Ana directed her light up through the shaft above her head. It reflected off the white marble of the inside of Rudolph Griffin's tomb. On the right wall of the tomb, she saw something that looked like a wide lever.

Ana lowered her head and shook it to keep from fainting. After stepping back, she sank to her knees, desperately trying to make sense of it all.

What is going on? Why in the world would you build this?

After several seconds, she lifted herself up and knew what she had to do.

"I've got to know!"

Holding the small, slender flashlight in her mouth, Ana put her trembling hands on the edge of the lid to the casket, hoping with all of her being that it was still locked.

"Come on, Ana. You can do this!"

She pushed and the lid yawned opened. Shaking all over, Ana removed the flashlight from her mouth, held her breath, and slowly peeked over the edge. The casket was empty.

Stunned and speechless, but at the same time also relieved that she didn't find the remains of Rudolph Griffin, Ana carefully closed the lid. Then she turned and raced back down the tunnel to the room with all the digging equipment. Once there, she closed the door behind her, locked it, and slid the skeleton key into her back pocket.

Completely numb from what she had just discovered, Ana made her way through the amazing folding shelf and left it standing open. She climbed the stone steps up to the ground floor landing. After closing the door to the hallway near the kitchen, she locked the dead bolt and put that key in her pocket, too. Turning around, she slowly made her way back down the steps to the cellar, crossed the floor, went back through the incredible, folding shelf door and closed it shut behind her.

"It feels like my heart is going to explode!" she cried as she made her way across the room to the tunnel that led to the massive metal door. Once through, she slammed it shut behind her. "No need to go back that way," she mumbled and then added, "ever."

Back in the large room, Ana shined her flashlight on the etching of a man's profile on the wall. "I can't believe it! Why didn't you let me know?" She turned and headed toward the secret entrance. As she walked along, she repeated the same question over and over. Finally, back at the creek, Ana crawled through the opening and closed the small, stone door behind her.

Ker-clunk!

Like in a fog, Ana made her way back up the stream toward her favorite spot. When she got there, she slumped down on the soft moss and stared at the creek. Holding her head in her hands, she began to cry. Ana sat completely still and watched the ripples in the water.

Why didn't you let me know?

Seconds ticked by. Suddenly her head shot up. "Wait a minute! You did let me know!" Ana sprang to her feet, yanked out her cell phone and opened the app with her photos. She scrolled down to the one she had made of Griffin's will in Dr. Barnes office. After using her fingers to enlarge the photo, she read the document slowly. "Oh, my goodness! There it is! There it is!" Ana read the words out loud, "I have buried my precious wife, Beatrice, and my dearest son, Lewis. I am ready to leave this place." Ana lowered her phone and exploded, "I am ready to leave this place! You didn't mean you were ready to die and leave this world, you meant you were ready to leave Lewistowne! Leave the mansion! Leave your old life and all the memories behind! You were ready to leave **this place**!"

In stunned silence, she stared aimlessly around at the natural beauty surrounding her. Ana shook her head, crammed her phone back into her pocket, and started making her way up the path toward the house. At the edge of the back yard, she spied her old play set. Ana walked over and sat down in the middle swing. For several moments she just stared at the grass in front of her. Slowly, she began moving back and forth, swinging and thinking.

You obviously had the mausoleum built after you learned that Beatrice was dying with cancer. But when did you start digging the tunnels? When did you come up with the idea to construct your 'coffin-lowering-I'm-leaving-this-place' contraption? How long did that take you? No wonder nobody saw you outside the estate. What a crazy, old stinker you were!

Suddenly, Ana slammed her feet to the ground and came to an abrupt halt. "Oh, my goodness!" She let go of the chain with her right hand and covered her mouth. "What if you're still alive?" she muttered. Ana glanced around to see if anyone else was in the yard. Satisfied that she was still completely alone, Ana let out a deep breath and slowly began swinging and breathing again.

And if you are still alive... where in the world are you?

One late summer afternoon, author J.W. Jenkins sat on his back porch, enjoying the company of one of his granddaughters. "She asked me to tell her a story, so I made one up. As the basic plot unfolded, I saw the reaction on her face and knew I had to write it down."

An avid painter, Jenkins also created most of the artwork in the *Ana Stilwell Series*. He and his wife, Pam, live in Newnan, Georgia.

Coming soon, Book #3 in the

Ana Stilwell Series...

ANa StilWell

The Light in the Tower

Would you like a free book?

We are offering the digital version of Book 1 of Dr. Tim Riordan's *Reading the Bible* series as a thank you gift. You will find this to be a useful companion to his other book on Psalms: *Songs from the Heart: Meeting with God in the Psalms.*

Accept your gift by visiting...

www.greentreepublishers.com/free-gift---psalms.html.

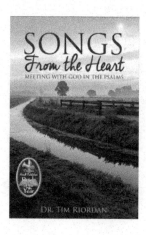

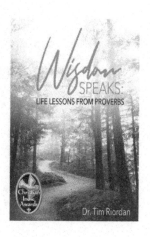

Help Children learn that they are stewards of the earth with "A Walk in the Woods."

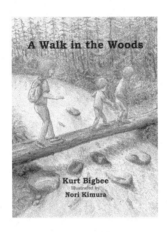

Wholesome Fiction for adults that's safe for the whole family...

You'll also enjoy this romance/suspense series from Judah Knight: The Davenport Series.